THE BOG BODY

W.A. Patterson

W.A. Patterson

The Bog Body

Chapter 1
Chapter 2
Chapter 3
Chapter 4
Chapter 5
Chapter 6
Chapter 7
Chapter 8
Chapter 9
Chapter 10
Chapter 11
Chapter 12
Chapter 13
Chapter 14
Chapter 15
Chapter 16
Chapter 17
Chapter 18
Chapter 19

W.A. Patterson

Other books by W.A. Patterson:-

The Tipperary Trilogy

- The Journeyman
- Safe Home
- The Devil's Own Luck

Thy Kingdom Come

The Bog Body

W.A. Patterson

The Bog Body

CHAPTER 1

It was late spring but winter hadn't yet relinquished its grip on the Irish countryside. In a desolate area of bogland outside the Tipperary village of Ballyanny, a young man shovelled the last spadeful of sodden turf into a hole. The past few months had been unusually wet, even by Irish standards, and the bog was not quite water and not quite earth. The cold night wind had a bite to it and although the rain was no more than a fine mist, it was unrelenting. The man's clothes were soaked through and sweat stung his eyes - not the thin perspiration that comes from exertion but the thick, greasy sweat that comes with sickness. He wiped it away with a wet sleeve. Grasping the spade in his hand, he looked down at his work.

'God forgive me,' he said, his voice low and tremulous. He looked heavenward. Tears ran down his face and mingled with the rain and sweat. He closed his eyes tight and begged the Lord for mercy, then he threw the spade as far as he could into the darkness.

*

Two women sat drinking tea in silence at the kitchen table. They couldn't have been more different in appearance. Una Murphy sat forward, her elbows on the table either side of her teacup, her chin in her hand. She was short in stature and somewhat portly. Her clothes were slightly out of style and she wore a pinafore apron over them, stretched tightly across her ample bosom. Una had long since abandoned any attempts to control her weight, having slid years ago into elasticated waists and waterfall cardigans. Una's best friend Joan Cahill sat opposite, perfectly upright with her back against the chair, her hands folded neatly in her lap. Joan was petite and well-groomed. Her carefully-chosen outfit was as stylish as her limited income would allow and, in contrast to Una's hastily-arranged mop of steel-grey curls, her hair was impeccably coiffed.

For forty-six years, Una Murphy had taught at Ballyanny's village school. Now she was retired, but her life of leisure was not of her own choosing. The Board of Management had thanked her kindly for her years of dedicated service, but had said it was time she stepped aside to make way for someone younger.

'Age discrimination!' she protested to anyone who'd listen. 'Just because your hair's grey, it doesn't mean you should be discarded like a loaf of mouldy bread!'

Joan had never worked a day in her life. She'd been privately educated in England where she met her husband-to-be while he was studying for his law degree. When Thomas passed the bar, they married and moved back to his native Ireland. Thomas secured a job in the conveyancing department of Griffiths and Company Solicitors in Thurles, and Joan kept house and hosted the odd dinner party for her husband's colleagues. It had been some years since Thomas Cahill's untimely death and the money they'd saved had slowly dwindled. Having been accustomed to the best of everything, Joan found it hard to adjust to life on a budget, but she did the best she could and she didn't complain. The two women lived directly across the road from one another and, over the years, had formed an enduring friendship. The bond

9

was strengthened by their mutual fondness for detective novels, in particular the mysteries of Agatha Christie.

'You wouldn't find her sitting around drinking tea,' grumbled Una. 'Something exciting was always happening in her world.'

Joan sipped her tea daintily from a cup and put it back in the saucer. 'Who are you talking about, my dear?'

'Miss Marple, of course.'

'Oh no, dear, Miss Marple led a dreadfully bothersome life. Why every time she turned around someone was being murdered. Imagine how ghastly that would be!'

'Well at least she didn't die of boredom.'

'Now don't be tiresome, Una. You know perfectly well that the kind of things Miss Marple got mixed up in don't happen in real life.' Una had just opened her mouth to protest when the kitchen door swung open.

'Shut that behind you, Aine!' called Una. 'You're letting all the heat out.'

'Jayzis, Nan, let me get me feet inside first!' A young woman in police uniform breezed into the kitchen, closing the door behind her.

'And wipe your feet,' Una told her.

Aine dutifully scuffed her feet on the doormat. She was a tall girl with an athletic build and the uniform suited her well. She took off the jacket, hung it on a peg behind the door and smiled at the two women as she rubbed her hands together to warm them.

'Is that tea hot, Nan?' she asked. 'I've been out in the freezing cold all day.'

'Of course it's hot,' snapped Una. 'What do you think we are, Yanks? As if I'd be serving cold tea!' She shuddered at the very thought.

Aine glanced at Joan and rolled her eyes. 'I see Nan's in rare form this evening.' She sat at the table and poured herself a cup of steaming hot tea from the pot.

'Anything interesting happening in the world of law enforcement, my dear?' asked Joan, changing the subject to avoid any potential disharmony.

The young Guard chose a custard cream from a small selection of biscuits on a plate and dunked it into her tea. Una shot her a withering look.

'Well,' she said, a sly smile playing around her lips, 'Sam McGinty's dog attacked one of Mrs. Kelly's chickens.' She pulled her biscuit out of the cup a well-practiced split second before half of it plopped into the tea. 'Oh, and a body was found in the bog.' She popped the soggy half into her mouth and glanced casually at her grandmother.

'Call that news?' snorted Una. 'Wait! What was that you said?'

Aine knew she had wrested the upper hand from her grandmother. 'I know, desperate isn't it? Seems the dog slipped its lead and...'

'Not the dog! The udder t'ing!' Una was always very careful with her diction, especially around Joan, but when excited she had a tendency towards the vulgate.

'You mean the chicken?' Aine was enjoying herself now. 'I'm afraid there's no hope....'

'THE BODY!' screamed Una.

'Oh that. Well, apparently old Jack Sheehan was out cutting turf and it seems he uncovered a head.'

'Was it attached to a body? Does anyone know who it is? Is it male or female?' Aine had Una's full attention now. She had known that her mystery-obsessed grandmother would be gripped by this tasty morsel.

'Slow down, Nan, we don't know much about it yet. They're bringing in an archeologist from Cork University tomorrow. We can't touch it until he carries out a full examination of the find...

antiquities and all that.' Aine was just about to dunk the remaining half of the biscuit into her tea when her grandmother snatched it out of her hand.

'Never mind that auld biscuit, pet, let me get you one of my scones. They're your favourite, I baked them fresh this morning. I'll make you a nice fresh pot of tea to go with it.'

'You do know, Nan, that if this turns into an active investigation I won't be able to discuss any of the details with you until after it's wrapped up.' As Aine suspected, her fleeting celebrity status melted away like a lump of lard in a hot frying pan.

'On second thoughts,' said Una, 'there's plenty of tea left in that pot, and you know where the scones are.'

'Ah come on now, Nan, you know the rules.' Aine helped herself to one of her grandmother's scones and slathered it with butter and strawberry jam. 'Anyway, it might not be a matter for the Gardaí at all. That body could have been there a couple of thousand years. I'm just saying, if we do get involved I'm not allowed to give out any information until the investigation is complete.'

'And as usual, Muggins here will be the last to know I suppose. No doubt by the time I get to find out anything, it'll be all over the Tipperary Star.' Una bristled with indignation but Aine knew that she was genuinely disappointed. Her grandmother had been delighted when she'd announced she was joining the Force, hoping that she'd be privy to exclusive information on all mysterious goings on. Joan did her best to defuse the tension.

'My dear,' she told Una, 'you can't expect Aine to jeopardise her career just to satisfy your morbid curiosity.'

'You mind yer own business, ya stuck up dryshite!' No sooner had the words escaped from Una's lips than she gasped and clapped her hands to her head. 'Joannie! I didn't mean that!'

A couple of seconds of silence ensued and it was as if everyone in the kitchen was frozen in time, then Joan began to laugh. Aine had been holding in a mouthful of scone but now she exploded into laughter too, spitting half the contents of her mouth over the tablecloth. Una, relieved that her friend hadn't taken offense, smiled as she handed Aine a plate.

'Here,' she said, 'you eat like you were expecting another famine.'

'I'll tell you what, Nan,' said Aine, 'why don't you come tomorrow morning? I'll try and get you as close to the scene as I can.' Una's eyes lit up. 'The archeologist will be there about nine. Bring Joan with you, but wear your wellies mind. It'll be filthy out there in the bog.'

All was forgiven. After sorting out the logistics for the morning, Aine went upstairs to change out of her uniform, Una began preparing dinner and Joan crossed the quiet village road back to her own house.

There was only the one road through Ballyanny, a sleepy village set deep in the Tipperary countryside, equidistant between Cashel and Thurles. Cashel of course was famous for its Rock, the former seat of Ireland's ancient High Kings. Thurles, although home of the GAA, Ireland's Gaelic games organisation, was probably best known for its gridlocked town square. Traffic congestion wasn't something the residents of Ballyanny had to worry about. The single road that ran the length of the village was so seldom travelled that one felt compelled to wave at every passing car. Chances were you knew the driver, and his wife, his children too, probably even his dog.

Of the three dozen or so homes, only a few had two storeys, the rest were single storey cottages. Although some of the older ones had been thatched at one time, the notion of idyllic Irish villages full of thatched cottages was now consigned mostly to postcards and biscuit tins. Today the walls were mostly white, or shades thereof, and the slate roofs grey. The Irish, although tenaciously independent, had a deep-seated sense of conformity and only the colour of the doors set the houses apart. Red ones, green ones, blue ones and even a yellow door or two provided variety and individuality to the villagers' homes.

There were two pubs, one either side of the village, where important matters of the day were discussed over a pint or three of the black stuff. Which Tipp team had the all-time best hurlers? Surely to God we'll bring home the Liam McCarthy Cup this year!

The church stood at the entrance to the village. Local legend told of it being built over an earlier thatched church which, in turn, had been built over an even earlier one and so on, like a Russian doll.

The bog was just south of the village. Although once the only source of fuel for the villagers, the use of turf for cooking and heating homes had all but gone the way of the donkey carts, much to the dismay of foreign tourists who came hoping to find the Ireland their ancestors left behind. Even so, on chilly nights like tonight, the sweet aroma of burning turf hung in the air, even if it did come in the form of briquettes purchased at the village store.

In Ballyanny, on this clear crisp night, everything was as it should be, but as Una Murphy peeled potatoes, her thoughts weighed heavy and her heart broke for the nameless soul buried in a bog down the road.

CHAPTER 2

After dinner Aine took a shower. She returned to the kitchen drying her wet hair with a towel to find her grandmother sitting at the table, riveted to the screen of her laptop.

'Not watching Corrie tonight, Nan?' Una never missed an episode of Coronation Street but the little television on its wall bracket in the corner showed no signs of life. 'You must be looking at something very interesting to miss your favourite soap.'

'Lemon drizzle,' said Una perfunctorily.

'You're looking at cake recipes? And there was me thinking you'd be researching bog bodies.'

'Oh I was, and then this popped up on the screen. Best Lemon Drizzle Cake in the World, it says. I couldn't help sneaking a quick look.'

'So have you learned anything?'

'About lemon drizzle cake or bog bodies?'

The Bog Body

Aine grinned. 'Well since we both know that Joan makes the best lemon drizzle cake in the world, I'll go with bog bodies.'

'Oh it's fascinating,' said Una, becoming animated. 'Did you know they were ritual sacrifices to the gods? It's true. They were murdered, most of them by being hit over the head and strangled... AND strangled if you please, as if being bashed over the head wasn't enough! The latest ones they found were about two thousand years old.'

Aine gave a low whistle. 'Now that's what I call a cold case.'

'Cold? Baltic more like!'

'Maybe you should stick to the case of the dog and the chicken, Nan, might be easier to solve. It is your first investigation, after all.'

'First investigation, indeed,' mumbled Una, pushing her chair back. She would finish washing the dishes and wait until Aine had gone before she resumed her research. 'I'm just interested, that's all. Anyway, I'd leave the whole dog and chicken debacle for the courts to deal with. The dog will probably plead temporary insanity anyway. His counsel will claim he had a difficult puppyhood, the judge will slap him on the paw and tell him not to do it again, and he'll trot straight out and kill another chicken.'

'Cynical,' sighed Aine, 'but all too true in reality. Anyway, I'll leave you to it, Nan, I'm off to watch the big telly in the parlour. Stay off those porn sites now.' She sprinted for the door but didn't quite make it before a wet dish cloth landed with a slap across the back of her neck.

'Aine Murphy, you've a mouth like a rugby fan!'

'I learned from the best,' laughed Aine. 'And I'm not a Murphy,' she called from the hallway, 'I'm a Gleeson, remember?'

'You're a Murphy through and through,' Una said to an empty kitchen, allowing herself a smile.

Although you wouldn't always know it from the way they spoke to one another, Una and Aine shared a very special relationship. They loved one another deeply, of that there was no doubt, but they shared a mutual respect and admiration too. The degree of separation in generation, and the unavoidable distance between Aine and her parents in Waterford, only served to strengthen the bond. Aine had moved in with her grandmother five years before when she'd graduated from Garda College and was posted to Cashel. Una saw much of herself in the bright and funny no-nonsense young woman. It was one of the reasons she was so fond of her. Their banter was just that, a playful exchange of words. Joan, with her English public school education and her Swiss finishing school etiquette, was appalled at their verbal abuse of one another but secretly, Una liked to shock her friend. In spite of her public persona, the straight-laced school teacher wasn't averse to a little mischief.

*

Already dressed in her uniform, Aine opened the door to Una's bedroom with a half-eaten piece of toast and jam in her mouth and a cup of tea in her hand.

She put the tea down on her grandmother's bedside table, then glanced out of the bedroom window and wrinkled her nose.

'You'd better bring a brolly with you today, Nan,' she said. 'It's raining.'

'When isn't it?' grumbled Una, tossing back her candlewick bedspread.

'Want some toast?'

'I'll make mine when I go down. I can't stand crumbs in the bed.'

When she arrived downstairs, Joan was already in the kitchen chatting to Aine. As usual, her friend's make-up was perfectly applied and her hair was immaculate, but this morning she appeared to be wearing a safari suit complete with belted jacket and matching slacks. Una rolled her eyes as she popped two pieces of bread into the toaster.

'It's quite the adventure, my dear, don't you think?' said Joan excitedly.

'Not in my book,' replied Una. 'Travelling to Venice on the Orient Express, that's an adventure, not sloshing around a bog in the rain.'

Joan had long since become impervious to her friend's brusque manner. 'I couldn't sleep with excitement last night!' she gushed. 'I got up in the end and made a lemon drizzle cake.'

Una had been leaning on the countertop waiting for her toast to pop up and Aine squeezed her shoulder making her wince.

'I was only after saying to Nan last night, Joan, your lemon drizzle is the best in the world. Wasn't I only after saying that to you last night, Nan?'

Una rubbed her shoulder. 'You have hands like hams, girl. That'll bruise.' The truth is Una was excited too, but she would never let on. She hadn't been able to sleep either. At last something different was happening in her humdrum existence. A bog body was a rare find in itself. To have one found buried outside their own little village was more than she could have hoped for.

The three women arrived at the scene with time to spare, although not before a mob of hopeful onlookers had gathered. News of the bog body had travelled fast and many of the locals had taken the day off work to be there. Local and national newspaper reporters were asking them inane questions and receiving equally inane responses which they scribbled down in their notebooks.

RTE had sent a van. A man with a video camera balanced on his shoulder filmed a roving reporter, a pretty young blonde who attempted to keep her hair from blowing into her face while trying to sound informed on the subject of bog bodies. Una recognised many of the words she used from her own internet search the night before, although lemon drizzle didn't get a mention.

The media were frantically trying to upstage one another, each desperate for a scoop. They scanned the crowd for anyone who stood out and Joan stood out like a sore thumb. The RTE blonde held back her hair with one hand and pushed a microphone into Joan's face with the other.

'Tell me, how do you feel about a bog body being found on your doorstep Mrs.... er?'

'Cahill,' replied Joan, taken by surprise. She smoothed back her hair and smiled sweetly at the camera. 'Joan Cahill.'

'Mrs. Cahill, tell our viewers what you think in your own words.' Joan looked over at the growing number of onlookers being herded into a corner of the field by what seemed like every police officer in Tipperary.

'I think….,' she hesitated. 'I think it would be the perfect day to rob a bank.'

The blonde didn't even hear Joan's response. 'And there you have it,' she said, 'direct from an inside source. This is Michelle McEnerny for RTE, live from Ballyanny in Tipperary.' She drew her hand across her throat to indicate to the camera man that the interview was over.

'And that, my dear,' said Una in a feigned English accent, 'is why we love you.'

'She's a lovely girl,' remarked Joan, 'just a tad on the dim side. Not to worry, she has her looks. She'll make some rich old man a fine wife someday.' Una sniggered, then realised that her friend wasn't joking. Just then, Aine returned from the grave site which had now been cordoned off with yellow crime tape.

'I've had a word with Detective Inspector Quinn,' she said. 'They've brought him in on the off chance this turns into a criminal investigation. He's a decent sort. He says you can both come as far as the tape, but no further... and you're not to touch anything or bother the archeologist when he arrives.' Una rolled her eyes. 'We have to treat it like a crime scene until we're told different, Nan, you're lucky to get anywhere near.'

'I'm no eejit,' snapped Una, 'I know how these things work. Haven't I been watching CSI on the telly for years?'

Nine o'clock came and went, then ten and still no sign of an archeologist. Finally, at half ten, a minibus pulled up and half a dozen young men and women piled out.

They donned what looked like white paper onesies and pulled blue paper booties on over their footwear. By now, Una and Joan had secured a vantage point at the perimeter of the taped-off area.

'No one told me it was a pajama party,' sniped Una, 'and how long do they think those paper boots are going to last in a bog?' Detective Inspector Quinn was standing just inside the tape and Una suddenly remembered that he was within earshot. She glanced up and saw him trying hard not to smile.

'They're archeology students, Mrs. Murphy,' he explained. 'They're going by the book. They don't know any better yet.'

Aine had liaised with DI Quinn on several occasions before; once when several items of agricultural equipment had been stolen from a local farm and once when thieves broke into the big house at Kilcooley and stole valuable paintings and antiques. They'd sat on the same table in the canteen a few times too and she liked him. He wasn't self-important like a lot of the detectives she'd met. She had introduced him to her grandmother when he'd allowed her and Joan near the crime scene. Una liked him too.

The students began lugging spades and sifting screens from the bus to the burial site, together with an array of cameras and electronic equipment. Their blue booties dissolved almost instantaneously and their white onesies were brown to the knees in no time, but their enthusiasm was unflinching.

'We got lost,' chirped the first fresh-faced lad as a Guard pulled up the tape to let them through.

Una snorted.' I doubt if any of that shower could find their arses with both hands.' Joan clapped her hands over her mouth at the vulgarity.

It was half an hour later when a black Range Rover pulled up and a short, stocky man got out. He sported a long, white beard and was wearing a trilby hat. He retrieved a pair of wellingtons from the back of the car and exchanged his brown brogues for them, then he put on a trench coat and pulled up the collar.

'Looks like Christmas has come early,' said Una in a low voice.

'And like Santy has joined the KGB,' replied Joan, giggling.

'That's Dr. O'Connor,' Quinn told them 'He's the Chief Archeologist and if there's a Santy at all, then O'Connor is the anti-Santy.' Joan hadn't meant for the Inspector to hear her and she blushed. 'There isn't a humorous bone in his body I'm afraid, ladies, so you'd be well-advised to keep the volume down on your observations.'

The archeologist made his way across the bog and ducked under the crime scene tape. Quinn extended his hand in greeting but O'Connor walked straight past.

He bent over the covered body and reached behind him. Without a word, one of his students handed him what looked like a small mason's trowel. He lifted the covering that had been placed over the victim's head and slowly scooped away a little of the peat. Silently, he passed the trowel back to the student and held out his hand again. Another student, a girl this time, gave him a soft paint brush. He threw it to the ground and snatched a whisk broom from her other hand. He swept away more loose peat revealing the victim's face. Una craned her neck to see. The skin was as brown as a chestnut. She knew immediately from her research the night before that it was due to the body having been immersed in the tannin-rich bog.

'Female,' O'Connor stated abruptly to no one in particular. 'Notice the absence of a supra orbital ridge.' He swept away more peat and peered closer as he scraped at something with the trowel, then he stood up and handed it back to the student.

'This is not an archeological site, Detective Inspector Quinn,' he said, brushing dirt from his coat. 'This is a crime scene.'

'Are you sure, Professor? Surely... well, you've only been here five min....'

'Whoever killed this woman used a lady's stocking to do it and unless I'm very much mistaken, the Druids didn't wear them. Also the body hasn't been here for any longer than seventy years and I'm almost sure that our ancestors had given up sacrificing humans by then. You'll see that I am correct when you have disinterred the subject. Her facial bones are largely intact and from an archeological standpoint, they would have degraded in the acidic water. Now if you'll excuse me, I have actual work to do.'

Quinn stood open-mouthed as O'Connor ducked back under the tape and walked off in the direction of his car. He hadn't seen this coming at all. He looked over to where a line of Guards were holding back a gaggle of reporters, all shouting questions. He sighed. 'A cold case so,' he said aloud to himself.

'Baltic,' came a voice from nearby. He looked up at the short, stout woman with the steel-grey curls and nodded gravely, then he walked slowly over to run the gauntlet of the press.

CHAPTER 3

DI Quinn spent ten minutes telling members of the press precisely nothing, fielding question after question with comments like 'I'm afraid I cannot comment on that at this time.' and 'We will release information as and when it becomes available.' Aine watched him as made his way back towards his car and she couldn't help thinking that he looked older than his thirty-six years. He caught her eye and motioned for her to walk with him.

'How long have you been on the Force now, Gleeson? Four years is it?'

'Five last January, sir.'

'Am I right in thinking you've never been involved with a homicide investigation before?'

'That's right, sir, I never have.'

'Well unless I'm very much mistaken, this one has all the ingredients of being a make or break case for a fine young officer like yourself, especially as you live in the village.'

'I'm... not sure I understand, sir.'

He smiled. 'Machiavellianism, Gleeson. Moving up the ladder in our line of work is all about politics and, more often than not, the road to advancement is littered with the bodies of our superiors.'

Aine was more confused than ever. 'I'm sorry, sir,' she said, 'I'm still not with you.'

'I expect this case to be high profile, especially if those jackals keep it running in the press, and I have no intention of giving them my head as a trophy for their wall. Are you ambitious, Gleeson?'

'Well, I....'

'Do you want to spend the rest of your career arresting drunken gombeens and handing out speeding tickets?'

'No, sir, in fact you might be surprised to know what my ambitions are.'

'Glad to hear it, nothing wrong with ambition. Here's what I want you to do. I want you to stay local and keep your eyes and ears open. You're to report anything out of the ordinary directly to me.'

'Am I to make enquiries, sir? The locals will talk to me.'

'Absolutely not, at least not for now. Those bloodhounds from the press might be watching and the last thing I want is for them to ride roughshod over my case.'

'I understand, sir, you can rely on me.'

'I hope so.' He smiled, catching Aine off guard. She dropped her gaze and found herself looking to see if he was wearing a wedding ring. He was. She blushed.

'I'm leaving a couple of uniformed officers here,' he told her, 'at least until forensics have had time to retrieve the body for the coroner. They'll be searching the site for evidence. It'll be good experience for you to watch them, I'm assigning you to guard duty.'

'Thank you for the opportunity, sir.'

He laughed. 'Save your thanks, Gleeson. If this all goes belly up, I'll be defending my job and you'll be spending the next twenty years walking the beat.' He ducked inside his car where he put in a call to the forensic team and wrote a brief report of the day's events for his superiors. Aine made her way back to the crime scene.

'I think a certain Detective Inspector has a soft spot for our Aine,' Una whispered to Joan. Joan smiled knowingly and nodded in agreement. Aine had walked up behind them and she'd heard her grandmother's comment.

'Don't be ridiculous,' she scoffed. 'Anyway, he's married.'

'No he's not,' replied Una with a smug grin.

'Yes he is, he's wearing a wedding ring.'

'Ah, well that's where you're wrong because it's not a wedding ring, it's a signet ring. He just wears it with the raised part turned inward. I shook his hand and I felt it against my palm.'

'That means nothing. Lots of men don't wear wedding rings these days and I don't even know why I'm discussing this with you.'

Una was undeterred. 'The knot in his tie is crooked too. There's a stain on his sleeve and his shirt has barely seen an iron. And he has odd socks on, I saw them when he took his wellies off. I'm telling you, that man has bachelor written all over him.'

'Your grandmother is right, Aine.' Joan jumped into the fray. 'I noticed stubble under his chin where he'd missed it shaving. No wife worth her salt would ever allow her husband out in public in such a state of disarray, especially where the press are involved.'

'Circumstantial evidence,' said Aine, waving a hand dismissively.

'But it's the preponderance of evidence, my dear,' protested Joan. She looked at Una in despair. 'I think we'll have to obtain a confession from the Inspector if we're going to convince her.'

'Don't you dare say a word, either of you! You'll only embarrass me, and yourselves.'

Joan put her hand on Aine's arm. 'It's impossible for your grandmother and I to embarrass ourselves, my dear. By the time ladies reach the age that we have, we're considered quite harmless. It's a misconception that provides one with the opportunity to do and say almost anything.'

It was a battle Aine knew she couldn't win. Retreat was her only option and she pulled away from Joan's gentle grasp.

'I'm on duty,' she said. 'Why don't the pair of you go and do the kind of things old ladies are supposed to do.' She strode off to take up her post near the grave and Una turned to Joan.

'We'll go home and put the kettle on, pet,' she said. 'We can discuss the merits of this case over a nice cuppa and a slice of that lemon drizzle cake of yours.'

*

The Bog Body

As they waited for the kettle to boil, Una swung the knitted tea cosy around in her hand.

'According to Billy Connolly,' she mused, 'you can't trust a man who, if left alone in a room with a tea cosy, doesn't put it on his head.'

Joan laughed. 'I love Billy Connolly,' she said. 'I had a major crush on him when I was young.'

'You? Billy Connolly? I thought you'd be more Roger Moore or Sean Connery.'

'Perhaps you don't know me as well as you think you do, Mrs. Murphy,' grinned Joan.

'Perhaps you're right. What do you think Detective Inspector Quinn would do if left alone with a tea cosy?' The two of them were still giggling as Una poured the tea.

'Now, let's get down to business,' said Una firmly, taking a notepad off the magnet board next to the phone. 'First things first. Victimology. We have to find out who the dead woman is before we can do anything else.' She wrote VICTIMOLOGY across the top of the pad and underlined it.

'Is that even a word?' asked Joan. 'I don't remember Agatha Christie ever using it in her novels.'

'Of course it's a word, it comes from the French *victimologie*. She said the word in an exaggerated French accent.

'What does it translate to?'

Una looked at her friend in disbelief. 'It translates to victimology, what do you think it translates to?'

Joan shook her head. 'How do we go about identifying the victim when we're not even sure when she died, or how old she was when she was killed?'

Joan was right. Even if the dead woman was local, the timeline mentioned by the archeologist was too vague. If they sifted through the Parish baptismal records, they'd end up with hundreds of names. Even if forensics narrowed down the timeframe and it turned out to be the 1930s, 40s or 50s, then they were talking about a period of economic hardship and mass emigration when the parish lost almost two thirds of its population. Locals, young and old, had simply upped sticks and left for a better life. Some had stayed in touch with family and friends but many had simply vanished, never to be heard of again. This was proving to be a lot more difficult than those TV crime dramas made out. They'd only just begun and already they'd hit a stumbling block.

The Bog Body

'Stay for dinner,' said Una. 'We'll see if Aine can throw any more light on it. I have to cook for her and me anyway. I'm roasting a lovely joint of bacon and we're having floury spuds and cabbage with it.'

'Why thank you, dear, I will. No cabbage for me though, it gives me dreadful wind.'

CHAPTER 4

It was seven thirty when Aine finally came home. Una and Joan were watching TV in the parlour and they heard her run straight upstairs. It was some time before she came down. Her lips were pulled tight against her teeth as she plopped into an armchair.

'Feckin' gobshite,' she snarled.

'Mind your language, girl,' scolded Una. 'Who's a feckin' gobshite?'

'Duffy. That fat tub of lard Quinn sent to partner me on guard duty today.'

'Why? What happened?'

'We were securing the perimeter of the crime scene together which meant us being in close contact and he thought it might be the perfect opportunity to try and rub his mickey up against me.' Joan gasped in horror. 'Not once mind. Twice, the lecherous little bollix.'

'Oh my dear,' said Joan, 'that's repugnant! That's sexual harassment in the workplace. I hope you reported him.'

'I threatened to but he just laughed, said the lads down at the station must be right in thinking that I bat for the other team.'

'You play cricket?' asked Joan, confused. She looked to Una for clarification.

'Joan, for the love of God, what planet have you been living on? The young ones use it to mean someone who's attracted to people of their own sex.' She turned to her granddaughter. 'I hope you gave yer man a mouthful!'

'I told him I was attracted to real men. I said that eliminated him.'

'Good for you. What did he say to that?'

'Nothing. He just wandered off. Said he was bursting for a piss and disappeared into the bushes. I wouldn't be at all surprised if he was feeding the donkey.'

'He's not all bad then,' offered Joan. 'At least he's kind to animals.' Her friend's naiveté was beginning to get on Una's nerves now. She put her hand up to Joan's ear and whispered something. The straight-laced Englishwoman's eyes widened and her jaw dropped.

'That's disgusting!'

Aine sighed. 'It's not just Duffy,' she said. 'There's always some cocky eejit waiting to chance his arm with a junior female officer. I wouldn't mind so much but he was gone for two hours and he stunk of beer when he got back.'

'Oh it gets worse,' protested Joan. 'You must report him, Aine.'

'There's no point. He'll only deny it and I'll be branded a whistle-blower. No officer snitches on another. It's like an unwritten law.'

'Well I don't blame you for being angry,' said Una. 'I'm livid myself and it wasn't even me it happened to.'

'What made it worse was that I needed a wee too, but I couldn't leave my post so I had to hold it in. I thought my bladder would explode by the time I got home.'

'Ach, I'm sorry you had such a bad day, pet.' Una got up and patted her granddaughter's arm. 'I'll put the kettle on and make you a nice cup of tea.' Tea was the answer to everything, the universal antidote of all Irish mammies and nannies. 'I've a lovely piece of bacon for your dinner, you'll feel better after a good feed.'

'Thanks, Nan, I'm starving. I could eat a reverend mother.' Una shot her granddaughter a disapproving glance but smiled to herself as she headed for the kitchen. She couldn't wait to ask about the investigation and the poor girl was only half way through her dinner when Una broached the subject.

'I've nothing new to tell you,' Aine said between mouthfuls. 'The wheels turn slowly in cases like this. The body's been taken to the coroner. He'll perform an autopsy to determine the cause of death and he'll look for clues as to the identity. The forensics team will be at the crime scene for a while. They've got to search the bog for evidence. It could take weeks and even then the body....'

'Stop calling her the body,' protested Una. 'The poor crathur was a person, a living breathing woman just like you or me or Joan here. She doesn't deserve to be dissected on some coroner's table. She deserves a proper burial in consecrated ground with a headstone to show somebody cares.'

'I agree, Nan, but like I said, these things take time. If it was up to DI Quinn the case would be treated as priority, but it's not his decision. These things are decided by people higher up the pay scale.'

'Doesn't make it right,' mumbled Una. 'Jesus, as if the poor woman hasn't been violated enough.' Aine was in total agreement with her grandmother but there was nothing she could do about it so she determined to change the subject.

'I was talking to Seamus Geraghty today,' she said, chewing on a large hunk of bacon.

'Well it must have been you doing all the talking,' replied Una, scowling at her granddaughter. 'I've never heard Seamie say more than a few words at a time... and don't talk with your mouth full! I taught his two children. Whenever him and Bridie came in on Parents' Day, she'd do all the talking and he'd sit beside her quiet as a church mouse. Mind you, he'd be lucky to get a word in with Bridie. God Almighty, what a chatterbox! She was a Foley before she married Seamus you know. The Foleys are all the same, lovely family but every one of them could talk for Ireland. There was a crowd of them here at one time. A lot moved to Manchester back in the sixties. I can't say I wasn't surprised when Bridie married Seamie, what with him being so quiet and her being so outgoing. Ah well, they say opposites attract don't they.'

'They do, Nan,' said Aine swallowing her last mouthful, 'and you're not wrong about Seamus. It's like he's in a world of his own half the time. I had to shout hello to him twice today before he even noticed I was there, and then he only touched the brim of his cap and nodded.'

'Always been the same,' said Una, beginning to clear the table, 'away with the faeries. His children were different altogether. Very popular at school, bright students too, both of them. I expect they get it from their mother. So when will the coroner have some answers for us?'

'Oh, it's us now is it? Listen, Nan, I doubt that I'll get to hear the outcome of the autopsy, and even if I do I won't be at liberty to discuss it with ye.'

Una was undeterred. 'I was thinking,' she said casually, 'once the autopsy report is in, I should invite that nice boss of yours to dinner. He'll be busy until then, I'm sure.' She reached for her granddaughter's plate but Aine held onto it and glared at her.

'Oh no you don't!' she said.

'But it's empty, pet. You've barely left the pattern on it.'

'I mean you're not to ask Quinn here.'

'How thrilling!' chimed in Joan. 'A delightful soiree with the lovely Detective Inspector! I'll bake a lemon drizzle cake for dessert.'

Aine shifted her glare to Joan and held it until the poor woman had to look away.

'You,' she scolded, 'are not Agatha Christie. And you...' she said pointing at Una, 'are not Jane Marple. You're a couple of old busybodies, that's what you are, and I'll thank ye to keep out of my work life, and my private life!' She got up from the table and marched up the stairs to her bedroom. They heard her door slam.

'Oh dear,' said Joan. 'That idea of ours didn't go down very well, did it?'

'Ah don't worry about Aine. I'll give her twenty minutes to calm down and then I'll take her a cuppa. If I go before that she'll bite my head off. If I wait any longer she'll harbour a grudge.'

'Well you know best, my dear, I'm off home. I'm at a loss when it comes to dealing with the younger generation, not having any grandchildren of my own, or children come to that.'

'They can be a trial alright, but they're a blessing at the same time. I wouldn't be without my Aine now, but I do live in hope that she'll have a family of her own one day. She'd like children; she said so when we sat talking one night. It's just a case of finding the right man.'

'Then we have two cases to solve, Mrs. Murphy,' said Joan with a conspiratorial smile. Una linked her friend's arm and walked her to the door.

CHAPTER 5

The body was taken to Limerick for a post-mortem. The coroner had been forced to use the Dissection Lab rather than the Pathology Department in order to accommodate all the observers. Forensic archeologists, pathologists and medical students alike had gathered, all eager to watch the proceedings. Even a priest attended which was unusual by normal standards. The case was gathering momentum and, even without a scrap of evidence, self-styled experts were offering their theories. It seemed that everyone had an opinion about the mysterious bog body, except those actively involved in the case. The public were devouring the story. The press was spoon-feeding them with groundless speculation and they were enjoying every delicious morsel. Even politicians were getting in on the act; any opportunity to get their faces in front of a camera.

The Bog Body

Under normal circumstances, DI Quinn would have been present at an autopsy but this was becoming increasing more like a circus than an investigation, a three-ring circus complete with clowns of which it was his misfortune to be ringmaster.

He made the decision not to attend and, after asking one of his men to keep him appraised of the coroner's findings, he headed back to Ballyanny. There wasn't much he could do there but at least it would remove him, albeit temporarily, from the chaos. In order for him to handle the cold case, he'd been seconded to the Serious Crime Review Team. They dealt with unresolved homicides in Ireland. The case was a complex one and pivotal to his career. If he messed this up he could quite easily find himself back in uniform and, after all the hard work and sacrifice it had taken him to get this far, that wasn't an option.

A misty rain was falling and the windscreen wipers clacked monotonously like a metronome as he left Limerick behind and headed over the border into Tipperary. Visions of the chestnut-skinned body swam before his eyes. Now and then the police radio crackled and a dispatcher would issue instructions to a patrol vehicle.

'Who are you?' he said out loud. 'Who killed you. Why did they want you dead?'

Hedgerows and scattered farmhouses finally gave way to the ribbon of roadside cottages that heralded the outskirts of Ballyanny. He passed the village church with its steeple that seemed to poke a hole in the clouds, then several more cottages before turning off the main road onto a muddy boreen that led to the bog.

A few members of the forensic team were still there dismantling a tent they'd erected. Quinn wanted to catch them before they left so he hurried over. He was hoping they had something for him but they'd found nothing. The case was already twenty-four hours in and he was no further forward. He noticed Aine standing on her own under an umbrella and he walked over.

'Where's Duffy?' he asked.

'He called in sick, sir, said he had the scutters. Sorry, sir, I mean diarrhoea.'

'Why don't you get yourself off home, Gleeson, get some dry clothes on.'

'Are you staying, sir?;

'Not for long, why?'

'I'll stay 'til you leave so? You can share my brolly.'

He laughed. 'As you wish, Aine.' It was the first time he'd called her by her first name. 'Well if we're going to be sharing an umbrella you can call me Gerard, while there's no one around that is.'

'Hardly anyone turned up today, sir, except for the last of the forensic team and a couple of reporters.'

'They're all in Limerick. They're like ghouls following the dead, and I said you could call me Gerard. Being called sir always makes me feel so old.' Aine was about to say something stupid about him not looking at all old when she was mercifully interrupted by the buzz of his mobile phone. He answered it and listened intently.

'Thanks,' he said, 'keep me informed of anything else that comes to light.' He tucked the phone back in his pocket and stared blankly into the distance. 'Interesting,' he said eventually, turning to Aine. 'The victim was still wearing both her stockings. The one they found around her neck hadn't been taken from her.'

'So the murderer could be a woman.'

'Don't jump to conclusions, Aine. All it tells us is that it's not one she was wearing. It could still belong to her.'

'Of course.' The sudden lowing of cattle distracted them both and they looked over to see a man driving a small herd of cows along the boreen. Aine raised her hand to him in greeting but he didn't return it, he just kept his animals moving forward.

'Who's that?' asked Quinn.

'That's Seamus Geraghty. He has a couple of smallholdings either side of the village. Once a week he takes his cows from one to the other.'

'Not a very friendly sort, is he.'

'Ah, it's just his way. My grandmother says he's away with the faeries.'

'Dairy farming's a tough old life. My father did it. He wanted me to take over when he retired but I had neither the desire nor the aptitude.' They watched as Seamus and his cows rounded a bend and disappeared out of sight.

'My father's a teacher,' Aine told him, 'that's how he met my mother. She teaches too, followed in Nan's footsteps. Her and Dad both work at the same school in Waterford where I come from.'

'It's in the blood so? I'm surprised you didn't go in for teaching yourself.'

'No thanks!' Aine shuddered.

'Well at least you'd be warm and dry instead of standing outside in the rain, ankle-deep in bogland. I don't know about you but I could do with a nice hot mug of tea. I think I'll head back to the station.'

The Bog Body

'If it's tea you're wanting, Nan's house is only up the road. She's always got the kettle on and she'd love to meet you properly. You're a real live detective and she's obsessed with crime dramas on the telly, reckons investigating murders must be the most exciting job in the world.'

Quinn laughed. 'Those dramas don't show you the reams of paperwork we have to trawl through and the endless reports we have to churn out. Thanks for the offer but I'd better get back to the office. Tell Mrs. Murphy I'll come for that cuppa soon. I'll tell her what being a detective is really like, see if I can cure her obsession.' He was still grinning as he made his way back to the car. He opened the door, then turned and waved. Aine waved back but he'd already ducked inside and closed the door.

She was sorry he hadn't taken her up on her offer but decided it was probably for the best. Nan might have tried to play matchmaker and she'd have been mortified. She started up the boreen towards home, dodging cowpats as she went.

When she arrived, she found her grandmother outside in the road shovelling dung into a wheelbarrow.

'That's the second time this week,' grumbled the old woman when she saw

Aine. 'It's bad enough he brings those cows of his through the village every Saturday, but here it is Wednesday and he's just been through again.'

'I know,' said Aine, 'I saw him. I waved but he ignored me.'

'Typical, tell me something new.'

'As a matter of fact, I do have something new to tell you. You know that stocking around the victim's neck...?'

Una shot bolt upright. 'What about it?'

'It wasn't one she'd been wearing.'

'How did you find that out?' She dropped the shovel into the wheelbarrow.

'Gerard Quinn told me. I've just been talking to him at the crime scene.'

'Ah it's Gerard now is it?' Una wiped her hands on her apron and grinned. 'C'mere, I'll go and dump this shit, you go and fetch Joan and we'll put the kettle on.'

*

Aine had to knock several times at the neat cottage door before Joan heard her. She'd been vacuuming the carpets for the second time that day. She would no doubt go over them again before the afternoon was out.

'Nan says you're to come over for a cuppa.'

'Two ticks,' chirped Joan. She considered leaving the vacuum cleaner in the middle of the floor but knew that she'd regret it. She liked to come home to a neat house so she put it away. She checked her reflection in the hall mirror.

'Oh I look a frightful state,' she groaned. She didn't. Aine thought Joan looked as if she'd just stepped off a front cover of The Lady magazine.

*

Una had been manoeuvring her wheelbarrow and its aromatic contents back around the side of the house when she heard the unmistakable plop-squeak of wellingtons on the road surface. She looked around to see Seamus Geraghty plodding back through the village, his collie dog at his heels. He wore a shabby flat cap and a brown canvas coat which draped over his hulking frame. Seamus had always been a big man but he was in his dotage now and he walked with a perpetual stoop. He almost always looked down at the ground when he walked and barely raised his head when addressed. Una dropped the handles of her wheelbarrow. She was going to give him a piece of her mind. She approached him but there was something odd about his expression. He tried to pretend he hadn't seen her but she stepped out in front of him, blocking his way.

'Everything alright, Seamus?'

'No, missus,' he said in a low voice. He didn't make eye contact with her but kept his eyes on the ground, as if searching for something he'd dropped. He stepped around her and continued on his way. Una considered following him and asking him to explain himself but decided against it. She wouldn't get a coherent answer anyway. Who knew what went on that fella's mind, if anything. She'd probably get more sense out of his dog.

CHAPTER 6

'I'm on lates starting tomorrow, Nan.'

'Late shift is it? You'll be back in the patrol car so. Does that mean they've wrapped up the investigation at the bog?'

'No. It just means they've finished collecting evidence. Forensics have to sift through it all now. It'll take weeks.'

'Weeks? Did you ever hear such nonsense, Joan? In CSI they just put whatever it is into a computer yoke and it spits out the answer in seconds. I suppose An Garda Síochána can't afford one.'

'There is no such computer, Nan,' sighed Aine. 'I keep telling you, CSI is fictional.'

'They have a different machine on Bones. It's better than the one on CSI. They put in all their findings and the next thing you know up pops a picture of the victim on a screen. We could do with one of those over here.'

'Bones is fictional too! There *is* no magic machine that churns out answers on demand.'

Una wasn't convinced. 'If they sent all the evidence to America, I'll bet those crime investigation people would have the case solved in no time.'

'Listen, Nan, we solve crimes here in exactly the same way as they do in the States, and it involves a lot more legwork and asking questions and fact-finding than it does laboratory analysis. All the facts are collected and logged and the evidence is gradually narrowed down.'

'Well it doesn't seem a very efficient way of going about things to me,' grumbled Una.

'Maybe not, but I'll let you into a little trade secret.' Aine had lowered her voice and the two older women leaned forward.

'Most cold cases,' she whispered, 'are solved through tip offs.'

Una was unimpressed. 'Well that's not how they do it on the telly.' She scowled and sat back in her chair, hiking up her bosom with folded arms.

'I'm sorry to burst your bubble, Nan, but that's how they do it in the real world. There's always someone out there with a guilty conscience, someone who knows something. The truth nags away at them and they need to get it off their chest, free themselves of it. Facts in a cold case are like pebbles in a stream. They start off as rough stones. Over the years they tumble along and become polished and eventually they turn to sand. It's a detective's job to gather together as much of that sand as he can and try to put the stone back together again.'

'But if that's the case,' said Joan, 'why even bother with the science?'

'Science has its place. It's there to corroborate the facts with hard evidence. People's memories alter over time, especially if the memory is painful. Over the years they forget. They remember snippets of facts and they fill in the blanks with whatever suits them, or whatever they can live with.'

'I see,' said Joan, 'so the science is there to separate the wheat from the chaff.'

'That's one way of putting it, yes. Our distant memories are a collection of half-truths and speculation. Over time it's like a stew that's been cooking for too long, it's hard to tell the turnips from the spuds.'

Una banged the flat of her palm on the kitchen table making Joan jump. 'It's all very well talking about stews and turnips and spuds, but in the meantime whoever murdered that poor woman is getting away with it. They have to be brought to justice. It's the least she deserves, that and a decent burial. Look at the poor unfortunate Magdelene Laundry victims, and all those little crathurs from the so-called Catholic Mother and Baby Homes. It's taken years for them to get the recognition they deserve, but still no one ever paid the price for their deaths.'

Aine knew that her grandmother was genuinely distressed and she put her hand on her arm. 'Don't worry, Nan. Everything possible is being done to find out what happened. If justice is to be had, we'll get it.'

'I wish I had your faith, girl.'

*

The following evening after Joan went home, Una sat by herself in the parlour. The TV droned on as usual but she felt restless and found it hard to concentrate, even on her favourite soaps. Una didn't like it when Aine was on late shift; the house felt empty with just her in it. As always, her armchair was positioned beside the window to make sure she didn't miss any goings on outside. She drew back the curtain to see what the weather was doing. The incessant rain they'd been experiencing for the last few days had abated now and thousands of stars dotted the firmament. A waxing crescent moon rose to greet them. Una felt she had to get out of the house. She went through to the kitchen and tested her torch to make sure the batteries were working.

'Don't want to break the auld neck,' she said out loud.

She pulled on a thick woolly cardigan that she kept on a hook beside the front door and donned a pair of wellingtons that had seen better days, then went outside. Unlike Joan's meticulously-tended flower borders and immaculate lawn, Una's front garden was unkempt. She liked to plant things and she liked to see them grow; she just didn't enjoy the maintenance side of things.

In the corner, several yellow roses and a clump of purple foxgloves jostled for position among a thicket of wild blackberries. Training the beam of her torch onto a path that led down the side of the house, Una made her way to the garden shed. She unhooked the corroded old hasp on the door and went in, rooting around for a while before she found what she was looking for.

Ah, there you are, she said to herself, extricating a pair of pruning shears from a jumble of rusty garden tools. She carried them back to the front garden, opening and closing them as she went in an attempt to loosen the hinge. *I think you could use a bit of oil*, she told them. *Your joints are as rusty as mine.* She snorted. *Jayzis, now I'm talking to a garden tool. I must be going in the head.*

She snipped off a few rose stems, pricking herself on a thorn in the process. She licked a tiny droplet of blood from her finger. In her apron pocket was a pair of old gardening gloves she'd found in the shed and she put them on. She cut some foxgloves and arranged them crudely in her hand with the roses. They looked lovely in the light that came from a nearby streetlamp.

Una looked over at her friend's house. The bedroom light was already on. Joan had a strict early-to-bed-early-to-rise regime, a habit she told Una she'd acquired as a young girl and one to which she attributed her good skin.

She opened the garden gate and stepped out, training her torch onto the road beyond. A pungent smell of cow dung permeated the damp night air, the legacy of Seamus

The Bog Body

Geraghty's cows. She followed what was left of their cowpats, like Hansel and Gretel following their trail of breadcrumbs through the woods, the beam from her torch dancing ahead. It seemed no time at all before she'd arrived at the bog. Without the village street lights, the bog was inky black. The wetland seemed to swallow up the light from the old woman's torch and regurgitate blackness. *What in God's name am I doing here*? she asked herself. Now she really did suspect she was going in the head.

She slipped and skidded down the embankment until her boots made contact with the sodden earth of the bog. She shone the light from her torch to and fro. The place seemed much bigger in the dark and a sense of foreboding hung in the air. It was exactly the kind of place that had inspired the ghost stories of her youth. *Nothing to fear*, she told herself without conviction. Disorientated in the darkness, she wandered about trying to get her bearings until she almost fell into the hole the body had been found in. Water from the bog had seeped in now, forming a pool of fetid sludge. Una shone her torch around the edge. The gravesite was much bigger than when she'd seen it last, thanks to the forensic technicians no doubt. She stood in reverent silence for a few minutes.

Who are you? Were we the same age, you and me? She tossed the bouquet into the putrid water. *I brought you these, and I'm going to pray for you.* She closed her eyes and was silent for a moment, then she began to pray aloud. She started with the Act of Contrition and continued seamlessly on to the Hail Mary. She blessed herself as she said the last line of the prayer.

'...now, and at the hour of our death. Amen.'

As she spoke the final word, she thought she heard something behind her. She dismissed it, putting it down to an overactive imagination, but then she heard it again. It was unmistakable this time. Una's nerves were already stretched as tightly as banjo strings and she froze on the spot.

'T'anks, missus,' said a soft voice in a thick accent.

Una was so startled that she dropped the torch. She lost her balance and was just about to fall into the hole when a pair of rough hands grabbed her shoulders.

The Bog Body

CHAPTER 7

'Seamus!' shrieked Una, clutching her chest. 'Mother of God, you scared the heart sideways in me!'

'Sorry, missus.'

'I nearly wet meself!'

'I'm sorry, missus,' repeated Seamus, bending down to pick up the torch. He handed it to her and she shone the beam onto his weathered face. He was gazing down into the watery grave. Although Seamus was seventy-five now, he was still a solid, thick-set build of a man, but as he stood with his back stooped and his brown canvas coat flapping around him in the night breeze, Una thought he looked frail somehow, broken. She touched his arm but he pulled away.

'I didn't mean ta scare ya, missus.'

'That's alright, Seamus, you just took me by surprise that's all. I was saying a Hail Mary for the poor crathur.'

'She'd like dat,' he said wistfully, still staring into the water-filled abyss. 'She'd like dem flowers too.'

His sorrow was palpable and Una suspected that he knew more. She was aware too that if she pushed him too hard he'd be gone. She was going to have to take it gently, like sneaking up on a hare that had already sensed her presence.

'I meant to say the Rosary,' she said, 'but I forgot to bring my beads.'

'I have mine.' He thrust a ham-sized hand into the pocket of his coat and Una slipped off her gardening gloves. When he pulled out an old set of rosary beads with the crucifix missing, she took them from him. Seamus removed his shabby flat cap and a breeze ruffled the white mane of hair beneath. 'Dey was hers,' he said, nodding in the direction of the pit.

Una almost lost her balance for the second time. She realised that here was someone who knew more about the identity of the body than anyone, certainly more than the police, but she was afraid to press Seamus further. She blessed herself and began to recite the Apostles' Creed aloud. Seamus didn't join in but when she glanced over she saw him mouthing the words. His big fist was clutching something that hung on a shoelace tied around his thick neck. When prayers were over, they both blessed themselves and she saw him tuck whatever it was back inside his shirt. She handed him back the rosary and saw that his sad blue eyes were brimming with tears. She felt like an intruder and looked away. To see a woman or a child cry was one thing; to see a big man cry was heartbreaking. Seamus coughed in an attempt to dislodge a lump from his throat and Una did the same.

'I'm t'ankful to ya, missus.' He coughed again to stop his deep baritone voice from cracking. 'T'was a kind t'ing ya did tonight. Auntie Kitty would be glad of it.'

'Not at all, Seamie, you're very welcome, and so is Auntie Kitty.' The batteries in Una's torch were dying and the light had turned a faded shade of yellow. She knew she had to get home before they went altogether, but an idea had popped into her head.

'I have to go now, Seamie,' she said, 'but if you want, we can say the Rosary again tomorrow night.'

'Ah I dunno....'

'That's alright. Well I'll be here if you change your mind. Good night, Seamus.'

'Good night, missus.' He nodded in Una's direction as she walked away, leaving him standing at the graveside staring in.

The old woman slogged laboriously back across the bog towards the embankment that formed the edge of the boreen. The sodden peat tugged at her wellingtons, trying in vain to pull them off, and each step was more difficult than the last.

The light from her torch was fading fast and what had started out as a brilliant white beam now gave barely enough light to see her way. She tapped the torch against her palm. It brightened slightly.

Hold out just a bit longer, she told it, *at least 'til we're on the road.* She laughed at herself. *First I'm talking to a pair of garden shears and now it's a torch. I'm definitely going in the head.*

The batteries finally gave out at the end of the boreen, just before she reached the road leading home. The welcome light from the street lamps now led the way, leaving her free to think about Seamus and the strange events of the evening. Poor Seamie. The villagers all thought him a quare hawk, a daft eejit, but Una's experience as a teacher led her to suspect that he suffered a degree of autism. The poor fellow was ill-equipped even to deal with everyday problems. If he was harbouring a dark secret, as Una suspected he was, it must be tearing the soul out of him.

What if he's the killer? She shook off the notion the second it entered her head and felt bad for even thinking it. *No, that's not it. It's not in the nature of someone like Seamus to be violent. Who's Kitty? Could it be Kathleen? Catherine perhaps. Auntie Kitty, he'd called her. That would have to be a sister of his mam or dad. God, I hope it's not just a family friend or I'll never be able to figure out who she is. Seamie knows, but how on earth do I get it out of him. Jesus, I need a cuppa.*

It was almost midnight when Aine got home. She found her grandmother sitting in the parlour with the big light off and the TV screen blank. Una glanced at her watch.

'You're late back,' she said.

'I thought you'd still be watching your crime dramas. You alright, Nan?'

'Me?' Una forced a smile. 'Ah sure I'm grand. Will I make you a cuppa?'

'Please, I'm gagging. Someone used the last teabag at work and they didn't get a new box in.'

'Typical,' said Una as she led the way back into the kitchen 'So, anything exciting happen in the world of law enforcement today?'

'Not much. Did anything exciting happen in the world of old age pensioners?'

'Not a thing.' Una thought this must be how a priest feels when he's told something momentous in a confessional box and can't tell anyone. She handed her granddaughter a cup of tea.

'Not having one yourself? asked Aine. Una shook her head. 'You're not watching telly, you're not drinking tea... Is something bothering you, Nan?'

'Ah no,' she said, unconvincingly. 'I was just thinking about that poor girl they found in the bog.'

'I almost forgot!' Aine spluttered on a mouthful of tea. 'That's why I'm late. Gerard called just before my shift ended. The autopsy results are in.'

Una shifted her weight forward in the chair. 'Maybe I will have that cup of tea after all.'

CHAPTER 8

Aine settled herself cross-legged on the parlour floor in front of her grandmother. She looked like a child waiting to be told a story, but it was she who had the story to tell. Una sipped her tea and tried to appear nonchalant.

'OK, Nan, so here's the lowdown on the dead woman. It seems she'd been in the bog for at least sixty years, seventy at the most, and they estimate her age at time of death somewhere between eighteen and thirty. She was about five foot four in height and they reckon she'd have weighed about a hundred and twenty pounds when she died. She had brown eyes with melanin in the iris, which would have made them hazel, and brown hair. But here's the interesting bit.. . she was two months pregnant.'

Una clapped her hand to her face. 'Pregnant? Do they know how she died?'

'Her neck was broken.'

'Does that account for the stocking around it?'

'No. The report said there was no subcutaneous hemorrhage which means that the stocking was never pulled tight.'

'How very odd. A stocking around her neck but no strangulation.'

'Gerard reckons the stocking could be a red herring. Or, he says, it could have been left there as some sort of token or message. I'm wondering if it was a murder at all, Nan. Maybe her death was an accident and someone tried to cover it up.'

Una narrowed her eyes. 'That's hardly likely. If it was an accident, why wouldn't whoever found her just report it? Why go to all the trouble of burying her body in a bog?'

'It's not as if they went to much trouble though, is it? All they needed was a spade and a convenient local bog. Anyway, folk didn't always trust the police back then.'

'A lot still don't,' scoffed Una. 'They've had their own fair share of scandals in the Force.'

'I suppose so. Anyway, I knew you wouldn't leave me alone until I'd told you the results of the autopsy but mind, you're to keep this to yourself. It's more than my job's worth to discuss cases outside of work and if I was found out... well, just keep it yourself, that's all.'

'Don't worry, pet, I won't breathe a word.' Una was tempted to tell her granddaughter about what had happened with Seamus earlier but decided against it. The last thing she wanted was for some heavy-handed detective to turn up at the poor man's house pressing him for information. Seamus would know she'd told them and then she'd never get anything out of him. It was time to change the subject.

'Have you any C-cell batteries, pet?'

'I do as it happens. Why? What's gone?'

'Ah the torch died a death. I thought I heard that auld cat up the road rummaging around in our bin again and I couldn't get the damn thing to work.'

'I have some spare ones upstairs, I'll go and get them.' Aine left the room and Una breathed a sigh of relief. She wasn't at all comfortable keeping secrets from her granddaughter but she mustn't betray Seamus' confidence, even if it was an unintentional one, especially if she wanted to find out what else he knew.

Aine returned with the batteries. 'There you go, Nan. Mind yourself out in the dark now, I don't want you taking a tumble.'

'Taking a....? I'm not geriatric, young lady! I might be the wrong side of seventy but I'm not decrepit, not yet anyway.'

Aine laughed. 'Good night, Nan,' she said. 'Sleep tight, and don't let the bedbugs bite.'

'I'll give you bedbugs!' her grandmother shouted after her in false indignation.

*

Una was in the kitchen making tea when Aine came down for breakfast.

'Will I boil you a couple of eggs, pet?'

'No thanks, I'll just have a piece of toast. I'm going into Thurles to do a bit of shopping this morning. Do you want to come?'

'No, I've got a few things I need to do here, but you can bring me back four chicken breasts from Hanlon's. I'll cook you something nice before you go to work tonight.'

'I'd love a curry.'

'Alright, well get some curry sauce while you're out too, not that powdered McDonnell's shite mind. It's vile.' Una disliked anything spicy but she often made a curry because she knew how much Aine loved it. She was convinced her granddaughter would eat it for breakfast if she served it up.

'I'll get a mild one, Korma maybe, and then you can have some too.' Aine stuffed the last of the toast in her mouth and took a gulp of tea before heading for the front door. Una clicked her tongue in disapproval.

'I've seen crocodiles eat with better manners.'

'Been watching David Attenborough again, Nan?' laughed Aine. She grabbed her coat and was out the door before Una could think of a sarcastic response.

'Always in a hurry, that girl,' the old woman grumbled. Just then the phone rang.

'Hello?'

'Can I speak to Aine please?' The voice was vaguely familiar.

'Who is this?'

'It's Inspector Quinn. Is that Mrs. Murphy?'

'It is and I'm sorry but you've just missed her. She's gone into Thurles.'

'Do you know if she'll be long?' Una sensed an urgency in the question.

'Not long, no. Is everything alright, Inspector?'

'Not really, Mrs. Murphy, they've pulled me off the bog body case. In fact they've dropped the case altogether, that's why I need to talk to Aine.'

'Dropped the case? But that doesn't make sense. Why would they...?'

'I wish I knew. I've just been to the morgue and the body's gone.'

'What do you mean, gone?'

'Just that, and there's no record of anyone signing it out, or even in for that matter.' Una was silent for a moment.

'Do you like curry, Inspector?'

'Curry?'

'Yes, Aine starts work at four today so we're having dinner early. If you like curry you can join us.'

'It happens to be one of my favourite things, Mrs. Murphy, so thank you, I will. What time?'

'Two o'clock alright with you?'

'Two's fine. Which is your house?'

'The first two-storey up from the church.'

'I'll see you later so.'

'Grand, and don't let on to Aine that I invited you. Bye now, bubye, bye, bye, byebyebyebyebye. She didn't give the Inspector an opportunity to ask why and, in the true Irish tradition of ending a telephone conversation, she continued her goodbyes until the receiver was back on the hook.

'Well,' she said out loud, 'the plot thickens.'

Una decided not to tell her granddaughter about their surprise dinner guest. If he just turned up, Aine wouldn't have a chance to scold her. She phoned Joan and asked her to come over. Even though they lived opposite each other, they often used the phone as a means of communication and, after all, there was no time to waste. Una had get the house ship-shape and Joan was much better at it than she was.

CHAPTER 9

When it came to housekeeping, Joan was a veritable genius and in less than two hours she had the cottage looking immaculate. Una was just putting the kettle on for the two friends to have tea when she heard her granddaughter come in. After hanging up her coat in the hall, Aine carried a couple of Dunne's shopping bags through to the kitchen. She stood looking around the spotless room with its uncluttered worktops and gleaming floor.

'Jayzus, are we expecting royalty?'

'Don't be bold. I've just had a bit of a tidy-up, that's all.' Una narrowed her eyes at Joan.

'A bit of a tidy up, is it? Looks more like the entire crew of Hoarders came while I was out.'

Una knew her granddaughter was right but she was indignant nonetheless. 'I'll have less of the lip thank you! Now go and change your clothes while I start dinner. Joan's eating with us.'

'Since when did we dress for dinner just because Joan's eating with us?'

'Look at the cut of you in those jeans and that horrible auld checked shirt.' Aine looked down at herself, bewildered.

'They're comfortable. What's wrong with them?'

'They make you look like a boy. What if someone came to dinner? That's no impression to be giving a person.' Una winced. She'd blown her cover and she knew it.

'Who's coming to dinner, Nan?' Aine asked, flatly.

When you get caught with crumbs around your mouth and your hand in the biscuit barrel, you've got two choices. You can either tell a lie, and it had better be a good one, or you can tell the truth and throw yourself on the mercy of the court. Una hesitated. She couldn't think of a lie, let alone a convincing one.

'I might have invited Inspector Quinn,' she mumbled.

'Jeeeeezus Christ, Nan!' Aine dropped the shopping bags onto the floor. 'What did you do that for?'

The Bog Body

'Don't raise your voice to me, young lady, and don't be using the Lord's name in vain. Anyway, it wasn't my idea.' There's the lie she'd been looking for. Granted it was thin, thinner than the skin of a sausage, but it might give her the upper hand.

'How does he even know where we live?' Aine's cheeks were blotched with crimson now and her hands were balled into fists.

'He's a detective, isn't he?'

'You told him. Ah Jeeeezus, Nan!' Aine turned and ran upstairs. They heard her bedroom door slam.

'I don't think she's very happy,' whispered Joan.

'Nothing gets past you does it, Miss Marple?'

*

The two friends were just put the finishing touches to dinner when a knock came to the door. They hadn't seen hide nor hair of Aine since the altercation earlier.

'I'll get it,' shouted Una, dashing into the hall with Joan at her heels.

'No you won't!' yelled Aine from upstairs. 'I'll get it!'

'I think she's still cross,' said Joan in a hushed tone.

'She'll be alright as long as he's here. I'll get both barrels when he's gone.'

They heard the bedroom door open and watched open-mouthed as Aine swept down the stairs like Scarlett O'Hara, a cornflower blue dress swishing about her legs.

'G'way!' she told them, flapping her hands and ushering them back towards the kitchen. She checked herself fleetingly in the hall mirror and reached the door just as another knock came. She opened it to find Gerard Quinn standing awkwardly outside, as rigid as if he had a broom handle stuck up his rear end, a bunch of supermarket flowers in his hand. The girl who'd answered the door was not one he'd been expecting and he opened and closed his mouth a few times but nothing came out.

'Are those for me?' She motioned towards the flowers. He'd forgotten he even had them and looked at them in surprise, as if they'd just appeared in his hand from nowhere. 'They're lovely,' she lied, taking them from him. Quinn mumbled something incoherent and Aine held them up to her nose. They smelt like the cheap perfume sold in euro shops. 'And they smell gorgeous too. Come in out of the cold. There's a roaring fire in the parlour.' She showed him through. 'I won't be long,' she said, 'I'm just going to put these in water.'

The two older women had been listening from the kitchen door and now they hurried back inside.

'Great idea of yours to make up the fire in there, Joanie,' whispered Una.

Joan smiled proudly. 'Well if nothing else, I do know how to set the stage.'

Aine entered the kitchen like a bride holding her bouquet, but her smile disappeared when she saw her grandmother.

'I'll deal with you later,' she hissed. She filled a jug with water and put the bouquet in it before joining their visitor in the parlour.

'Oh dear,' groaned Una, 'I'm for it.'

'I'll hide the knives after dinner,' said Joan. 'I wouldn't want them taken away as exhibits in a murder trial.'

*

'Did your grandmother tell you about the case being quashed?' Gerard stood with his back to the open fire. 'I called this morning and asked her to tell you.'

'What? No.' What else hadn't her grandmother told her?

He relayed to her what he'd told Una on the phone and Aine listened attentively.

'Cover up?' she asked, when he'd finished.

'Stinks of it.'

'Who can even do that?'

'I don't know, but whoever it is has some serious clout.' Just then, Una poked her head around the door.

'Dinner's ready.'

Dinner was an exercise in mortification for Aine. Gerard underwent a gruelling interrogation about his private life although, to Aine's surprise, it was Joan who did the cross examination and to be fair, the way she went about it, he probably thought he'd volunteered the information. Her grandmother ate in relative silence; she even appeared somewhat disinterested in what the Inspector had to say. What Aine didn't know was that Joan had been appointed as Chief Inquisitor by Una.

They discovered that Gerard had been married, but that he and his wife had divorced some years before. Evidently he blamed himself for the breakup, saying he'd spent more time building his career than he had working on his marriage. He visited his eight year-old daughter on the few weekends that he wasn't on duty and, like most estranged parents, he spoiled her rotten when they were together. It was a common occurrence that Una had seen time and time again with the children she'd taught. She believed it to be overcompensation brought on by a guilty conscience for the parent's perceived failure.

Una kept an eye on the kitchen clock. She knew that Aine had to leave for work at half three and she calculated that if it took her fifteen minutes to get ready, then Gerard would have to be kept talking until at least a quarter past if she was to avoid being left on her own with her granddaughter. Again, that would be Joan's job. She was far more accomplished in the art of polite conversation so whenever the conversation flagged, Una gave her friend a little kick under the table at which point she would adeptly introduce a new topic. Joan kept herself abreast of current affairs, she was interested in most sports and was well-read. She was able to discuss most subjects with ease and knowledge. It was one of the things that Una loved about her, that and her unquestioning loyalty. Joan was an excellent and dependable friend. Three fifteen came around.

'You should be thinking about getting ready for work, pet,' she said, with uncharacteristic timidity. Gerard looked at his watch.

'God, is it that time already?' he said, standing. 'I'm sorry, I've outstayed my welcome.'

'Not at all, Inspector. We've enjoyed the afternoon immensely, haven't we Aine?'

'Immensely,' repeated Aine, frowning at her grandmother.

'It's usually takeouts for me,' he laughed. 'That's the first home-cooked meal I've had in months. Thanks very much for inviting me.'

'We have a roast on a Sunday,' said Una. 'If you can be here at four there'll be a place set for you.' She daren't look at her granddaughter.

'Well that's very kind of you, Mrs. Murphy, I'd love to. I'll clear my busy social calendar and I'll be here at four on Sunday.' He shook her hand, then he took Joan's and kissed it. Joan blushed and tittered like a schoolgirl. He turned to Aine and his first reaction was to kiss her cheek but he caught himself. 'If I haven't told you already,' he said, 'you look lovely. Don't worry, I'll see myself out.' With that he was gone and the three women were left standing in the kitchen looking at each other. Aine scowled at her grandmother.

'Well, if you and your accomplice here have quite finished humiliating me, I'll go and change for work.' She stood up and was about to head upstairs when Una spoke.

'Her name was Kitty?' Aine stopped in her tracks and turned around.

'Whose name?'

'The woman they found in the bog. Her name was Kitty.'

CHAPTER 10

'Is this some pathetic attempt at worming your way out of trouble?' said Aine, glaring at her grandmother.

'Now just a minute, young lady. Exactly what trouble am I supposed to be in?'

'You know what I'm talking about, inviting my boss to supper without telling me.'

'Is that all? Why, didn't you enjoy his company?'

'I wanted to crawl under the table with embarrassment... but I enjoyed his company, yes.'

'Well he must have enjoyed yours because he's coming back on Sunday.'

'Only because you ordered him to!'

'Nonsense. A Detective Inspector tells other people what to do; he's not about to take orders from an old age pensioner.' Aine felt herself losing ground. She was on thin ice and she could almost hear it cracking beneath her.

The Bog Body

'Why didn't you tell me the bog body case was closed? I felt like a proper eejit.'

'I thought it was better coming from him. Did you want him to think you'd been discussing one of your cases with your grandmother?' The ice gave way now and Aine found herself thrashing around in frigid water. She glanced at the kitchen clock.

'Jesus, I'll be late. I have to get changed yet.' She ran upstairs. 'I'm not done with you yet though!' she yelled. Una shrugged her shoulders.

Ten minutes later Aine returned in full uniform, all traces of make-up removed from her face.

'By the way,' she said, 'I put the batteries in that torch. If you do have to chase off any cats in the dark tonight, mind you don't take a tumble.' She slammed the door behind her, leaving her grandmother fuming at the inference.

*

Una kept an eye on the clock and when seven finally came around, she put on her big woolly cardigan and rummaged around in one of the pockets to make sure she had the rosary beads. She wished she had one of those voice recording machines, although she'd be terrified that Seamus would hear it whirring. If he was going to share any dark secrets from the past, the last thing he'd want was for her to be recording them for posterity. She slipped into her wellingtons and snatched the torch from the shelf.

When she arrived at the bog she could see Seamie's silhouette already beside the grave. The ground beneath her seemed even more water-logged than it had the night before and it took her longer to reach him. With every footfall her wellingtons made a squishing sound, then a sucking sound as she pulled them out. When she finally got there, she found him staring into the dark pool.

'I t'ought ya might of fergot,' he said without looking up.

'I didn't forget, Seamie.' Una decided to chance her arm. She took the rosary from her pocket and blessed herself. 'Dear Lord, we dedicate our prayers to... is it Kathleen, Seamie?' He nodded. 'And what's her last name?' He threw her a sideways glance. 'There's an awful lot of Kathleens in heaven,' she told him. 'We wouldn't want the wrong one to get your Auntie's prayers.'

The Bog Body

He hesitated. 'Egan,' he said, finally, 'same as Mammy, God rest 'er soul. Dey w's sisters.'

Una kissed the crucifix. Seamus unbuttoned his collar and pulled at the string around his neck with his big hand. He grasped whatever was hanging on it.

'What is that, Seamie?'

Slowly he opened his hand to reveal something shiny and oval-shaped. Una instantly recognised it as a Miraculous Medal. She knew without looking closer that it had the Blessed Virgin Mary embossed on it and the words, 'O Mary, conceived without sin, pray for us who have recourse to thee.' encircled around her. To those who wore it, it was a testimony of their faith and their trust in the power of prayer.

'D' chain broke ages ago,' he told her. 'I kept meanin' to get it fixed but I kept fergett'n. Now I can't find it at all so I have it on dis auld shoelace.'

'It's very pretty,' said Una tenderly, as if talking to a child.

'She was pretty.' He nodded towards the grave. 'She gave me dis fer me fift' birt'day.'

'That was very kind of her. When was that, Seamie?' Una was trying to establish a timeline.

'I told ya,' he said with a slight edge to his voice, 'me fift' birt'day. I was born twenty-eigh' day of April nineteen forty-t'ree.' He announced his date of birth mechanically, as if he'd been taught it parrot-fashion, then he dropped his head. 'Auntie Kitty disappeared two days after.' He corrected himself. 'No, t'ree days after.' He wiped his eyes with the back of his hand. 'Some t'ings I remember, missus. Some t'ings I don't want ta.'

Una did a quick calculation in her head. Kitty had disappeared in 1948. She decided not to push Seamus any further for fear of him shutting down and locking forever the door to the past. She made the sign of the cross and began.

'I believe in God, the Father Almighty, Creator of heaven and earth....'

When prayers were finished, they both blessed themselves.

'Same time tomorrow, Seamie?' Seamus hesitated.

'I dunno, missus. Some t'ings are best left dead an' buried.'

'Well I'll be here,' she said,' it's the least I can do for the poor woman.' She added the last part to bait him. 'Good night, Seamus.'

'Night, missus. Well, I might see ya tomorra so.'

The Bog Body

She had set the hook. Now all she had to do was play the fish and land it.

*

Una was waiting in the kitchen when her granddaughter returned home from work.

'How was your day, pet?' she asked casually.

'Don't you 'pet' me.'

'Still in a bad mood, I see?'

'Do you blame me? Now spill the beans, Nan, I want you to tell me everything you know.'

'Let me at least make you a cuppa first.'

'I'll make my own tea. You talk.' Una sat at the table while Aine switched on the electric kettle and got a mug down from a cupboard. She took a breath and told her granddaughter everything she knew in one go.

'Her name was Kathleen Egan but people called her Kitty and she disappeared on the first day of May, 1948.'

'Is that everything?'

'That's everything.'

'And who's your source?'

'Ah now I can't tell you that, pet, not yet anyhow.'

'You can't or you won't?'

'Let's just say it would be a sin to betray the trust of an innocent person.'

'And it's a crime to pervert the course of justice!' Aine's last statement was too much for Una.

'Don't you talk to me about perverting the course of justice,' she snapped. 'not when some top dog in An Garda Síochána has the case shut down altogether and the body whisked away as if it never existed. How is that justice, I'd like to know?'

'I need to phone Gerard, he has to know.'

'I wouldn't if I were you,' warned Una, 'not if you value your job, and his come to that. I'd strongly advise you to keep this under your hat, at least for the time being.'

'Why? What do you mean?'

'If a case is closed down and a body disappears, then whoever's responsible must have a lot of clout. They must be afraid of something too and that means they have something to hide. Trust me on this one, Aine, say nothing.' Aine sat down and looked at her grandmother.

'Someone that powerful with something to hide could be dangerous.'

'Not necessarily, they're like cockroaches. They lurk in the shadows. I intend to shine a light on them and watch them scurry out.'

'You be careful, Nan.'

Una laughed. 'Now who in the world is going to suspect an old woman and her equally old friend?'

'You could be opening a Pandora's box and God only knows what's inside.'

'That's precisely why I want to protect you, and your boyfriend.'

'Gerard is NOT my boyfriend.'

'Not yet, anyway. Enjoy your tea, it's past my bedtime.'

'God, you're infuriating, Nan!'

'I know. Good night, pet.'

CHAPTER 11

Una yelled up the staircase. 'Aine! Me and Joan are going into Thurles! Do you want anything?' Aine half opened her bedroom door and poked her head out.

'I went yesterday!' she yelled back. 'Why didn't you come with me then?'

'Because I didn't know what I wanted yesterday!' Una grinned at Joan.

'Alright, well don't be spending too much on me!' Aine was grinning now too. 'You can't get around me with expensive gifts, you know!'

'That's a shame! I'd planned to spend the life savings on you today!'

'Well in that case, I'm open to bribes!'

Such was the relationship between Una and her granddaughter. They were more alike than either of them cared to admit and, whenever conflict did arise, it was cultural and generational. The old woman could be cantankerous, the young one stubborn and, like flint striking against steel, on the occasions that they did clash, sparks were bound to fly. Their bond, however, was unbreakable. It might stretch now and then, sometimes to near breaking point, but it never did break and it was always quick to snap back into place.

Una was glad that the young women of today enjoyed more freedom than she'd had. When she was Aine's age, opportunities for women had been limited. It was automatically assumed that a girl would marry, have children, then stay at home and look after them. As far as professions went, becoming a schoolteacher, shopkeeper or nurse were pretty much the only options on the table. If a girl did aspire to any other career, it was almost always just a pipe dream. Aine lived in a different world. Although the possibilities for women weren't yet endless, the range of opportunities was constantly becoming wider. Even though it was still a man's world, the walls of convention were coming down and young women weren't suffering the constraints that had stifled generations of their gender before them. Aine had talked about the possibility of settling down one day and having a family, but she wasn't about to give up her career for it anytime soon, if ever. Far from begrudging her granddaughter the freedom to decide her own future, Una was glad for her.

*

Joan was driving. She parked in one of the town's Pay and Display car parks and left Una in the car while she went to get a ticket from the machine. She came back and placed the ticket on her dashboard where the parking attendant could see it.

'I paid for four hours,' she said, reminding Una why she disliked coming into town with her friend. Joan could spend hours browsing the boutiques. She knew the staff well enough in most shops to be greeted with a kiss on the cheek and she would take item after item of clothing off the racks and hold them up to see how she'd look. She kept herself abreast of all the latest fashions and she knew what all the celebrities were wearing. Una couldn't care less. She liked to go where she needed to go, get what she needed to get, then go home. After three hours of traipsing around behind Joan, she'd had enough.

'Let's eat,' she said. 'I could eat a badger's arse through a hedge.'

'Really, Una!' The two women had been best friends for years but on occasion, Una's vocabulary still horrified the well-bred

The Bog Body

English woman. 'Very well, we'll have a bite to eat at that quaint little Tea Rooms in Abbey Street. They have the most scrumptious cupcakes there.'

'I prefer Gráinne's, she serves proper food.'

'Splendid idea! There's a darling little dress shop a few doors away, I might just pop my head in the door before lunch. You will come with me won't you, dear.' Una rolled her eyes so far back in her head that she thought she saw her brain.

'Of course,' she said. 'I haven't had this much fun since I had all me teeth taken out.'

'You are a card,' giggled Joan.

Una managed to sneak out of the dress shop while Joan was discussing a rack of blouses with the owner, blouse by blouse. She headed down the street to a jeweller's shop and, as she entered, a bell tinkled over the door. A wizened old man with a neck like a chicken stood behind a glass-topped counter.

'Can I help ya?' he asked.

'I need a silver chain.'

'Fer yerself is it?'

'No, it's for a friend.'

'How big is yer friend's neck?'

Una made a circle with her hands, hesitated, then opened them further.

'Jayzus, is yer friend human?' The shopkeeper laughed but Una glared at him and he cleared his throat. 'Well now, I'd say dat's about t'irty inches. I have a selection.' He pointed to where various designs of chain sat side by side in rolls, wrapped around spools. 'Dis one's lovely.' He caught the end of a chain and pulled it out to display it on the palm of his hand. 'Seven euro an inch.'

'He's not that good a friend.'

'How about dis one.' He pulled out another chain. 'Five euro fifty.'

'Haven't you anything cheaper? He's really more of an acquaintance than anything. What about that one on the end? It says one euro.'

The shopkeeper was deflated. 'Silver plate,' he said, 'over base metal.'

'I'll take it.'

The old man measured off thirty inches then, using a jeweller's loupe, he attached a clasp. He put the chain on a bed of cotton wool in a small box and pushed the box towards Una on the glass counter top. He kept his finger on it.

'Dat'll be t'irty-five euro,' he said.

'I thought it was one euro an inch.'

'It is; the clasp is real silver.'

The Bog Body

Una stared at him and he stared back, his finger still on the box. Finally, she relented and handed him two twenty euro notes. He pulled the lever on the side of an antiquated cash register and the drawer opened with a clang. He handed Una her change and put the little box into a bag.

'How much is the bag?' she asked, sarcastically.

'The bag's free.' He grinned a yellow, snaggletooth grin. 'I hope your acquaintance likes his chain.'

Una found Joan waiting outside the dress shop. They went into Grainne's together and, once they'd settled themselves at a table by the window, Una showed her purchase to her friend. Joan took the chain and weighed it in her hand.

'You know this is silver plate?' she said.

'I know, over base metal apparently.'

'How much did you pay for it?'

'One euro an inch.'

'You know that dress shop I was just in?'

'What about it?'

'They have the same design for half the price.'

'Now she tells me. My day just gets worse.'

*

Una's day was to worsen still. She left the house at seven o'clock and made her way down to the bog. She had high expectations of Seamus tonight and was looking forward to finding out more about Kitty. When she arrived, however, there was no silhouette up ahead. Somehow the bog seemed darker and more sinister than it had on the previous nights and she considered going home. In spite of her trepidation, she decided she'd come this far so she might as well carry on to the gravesite and say a Rosary for Kitty. Without Seamie's outline to guide her, it took her ten long minutes to find it.

'Well, Kathleen,' she said aloud when she arrived, 'it looks like it's just me and you tonight, pet. If only you could tell me what happened. Why would someone take your future away? What were they afraid of? I can't help you, not without Seamie's help anyway, but I can pray for your soul.'

She pulled out her beads, kissed the crucifix and began. She was on the final decade when she heard the sound of a tractor engine coming from the boreen. She recognised the growl and clank of Seamie's old diesel Fordson and she shone the beam of her torch in the direction of the noise.

The Bog Body

Almost before the tractor ground to a halt, Seamus jumped off and ran over to her. It took him a while to catch his breath.

'I wasn't goin' ta come,' he gasped. 'I wasn't goin' ta come but I was in me barn and I heard a voice.' His chest heaved from the exertion. 'It said I had to finish da story. It said if I didn't finish, I'd never get any peace.'

Despite the inky darkness that surrounded them, Una's day had begun to grow a little brighter.

CHAPTER 12

'Everyone says I'm t'ick, missus.'

'Oh I'm sure that's not true, Seamie,' Una lied.

'I don't blame 'em. I can't read. I tried mind. Me Da said I had to help him on da farm so I only went ta school fer two years, but I tried. I just kept gettin' all me words jumbled up.'

'That's not being thick, Seamus, that's just a learning difficulty that some people are born with. It's called dyslexia, it doesn't mean you're stupid.'

'Ah sure I hated school anyway. Da kids called me names and there w's too much noise. Too many people.' He knuckled his forehead to emphasise the point. 'Made me brain hurt. But I remember t'ings.' He tapped a gnarled finger to his temple now. 'I can't write t'ings down but I can keep 'em in me head.'

'Do you remember your Auntie Kitty?'

He smiled and his eyes softened. 'Ah I do.'

The Bog Body

'What makes you think it's her they found here?'

'Sometimes I just know t'ings. I know it's her.'

'Tell me about her. Did she have a sweetheart?'

'Tommy Riordan.' Seamus was grinning now. 'Ah sure Tommy w's a gas fella altogether. Alw's laughin' and jokin'. Him and Auntie Kitty w's sweethearts ever since school. We all t'aut dey'd wed but den Auntie Kitty finished wit' him. Just like dat, outta da blue, a couple o' mont's before she went away.' The smile slid from Seamus' face. 'Tommy didn't laugh and joke any more after dat. Broke his heart it did.'

Una knew from watching her crime dramas that unrequited love had the habit of turning deadly. Jilted lovers were always high on the suspect list.

'Do you think Tommy had anything to do with your Aunt disappearing?' she asked. Seamus shook his head vigorously.

'Oh no, missus, not Tommy. After she went he came to our house every week ta see if we'd heard from her. He never wed, he waited fer her 'til d' day he died.'

'Tell me about the last you time saw her. Do you remember?' Seamus nodded. His eyes glazed over and he stared over Una's shoulder into the distance. She didn't rush him. She knew he was travelling back in time to his five year-old self.

'Dey had a bust up,' he said. 'Her and Mam. I never seen 'em fight before, ever. Auntie Kitty told Mam she w's in trouble and said she had ta go away.'

He looked at Una. 'I know about dat sorta trouble now, missus. I didn't back den. Mam begged her to stay but she said she didn't want ta end up in one o' dem laundries. She said she w's goin' to England. She w's to meet him at da church and dey w's goin' togedder.'

'Him? Did she say who she was meeting?' Seamus shook his head.

'No. Da fadder I suppose.'

'And she didn't say who the father was?' Again, he shook his head.

'Do you remember anything else, Seamie?'

'I remember her and Mam cryin'. Dey hugged and dey cried and cried. I cried too. I didn't know why I w's cryin', I just knew somet'n bad w's happenin'. Auntie Kitty ran out and I never seen her again. I seen her when dey dug her up, but I don't want ta remember her like dat. I ain't slept since dey found her, missus.'

Una wanted to comfort him, but she knew he'd be horrified if she tried to touch him. She reached into her pocket.

'Here,' she said. 'I have something for you.'

'Fer me?'

'Yes, I got you a present. Here.' She held out the little box. He looked at it and took half a step back. She opened it. 'You said you lost the chain for your medal. I got you a new one.'

'What would you be gettin' me a present fer?'

She'd made him suspicious and she knew that if she was to keep him on her side, she had to gain his trust. She had to make a connection with him, so she told a white lie.

'You said you hated school because they called you names.' He nodded. 'Well I'll tell you a secret. They called me names at school too. I was fat and they used to oink and grunt at me. They called me Miss Piggy.'

'Miss Piggy?' The barest of smiles touched his lips. 'Like in da Muppets?'

'That's right, like in the Muppets, only I was Miss Piggy before she came along.'

'Dem Muppets make me laugh. I used to watch 'em all da time wit' me kids.'

'I taught your children, Seamie.'

'I know. I w's alw'ys scared o' ya.'

'Scared of me?' Una laughed. 'Now who could be scared of Miss Piggy?' The ice was broken. He took the chain from the box and held it up in the dim reflected torchlight, then he reached inside his shirt and pulled out the medal.

'Dis auld shoelace has bin tied around me troath fer years. I don't t'ink da knot'll ever undo.' He reached deep into the pocket of his canvas coat and pulled out a large folding knife. It was Una's turn to step back now as he expertly flipped open the blade. It suddenly occurred to her that she was alone at night in a bog with a large, somewhat simple, knife-wielding man. She exhaled audibly as he offered it to her handle first.

'Will ya cut it fer me, missus?' Una took the knife and sawed through the shoelace. It was as tough as wire after being around his neck for so long. Seamus fumbled with the chain as he tried to feed the medal onto it.

'Ah here,' she said, 'you have fingers like sausages. Give it to me before you drop it. We'd never find it in this.' Her tone was that of a schoolteacher talking to a pupil and Seamus dutifully handed her the medal. She fumbled with it too which made Seamus laugh.

'I haven't got me glasses with me, ' protested Una. Finally, she managed to thread the chain through the bail. 'There!' she said, 'I've done it. Now bend forward so I can put it around your neck.' Seamus complied and she reached around him. 'Jesus, Seamie, your neck must be as thick as my waist!'

Seamus looked down at her waist and Una found herself involuntarily sucking in her stomach. It was like shovelling water.

'Ah no, I wouldn't say so, missus.'

'Humph,' she grunted.

'Ya know, it's funny,' said Seamus clutching the medal in his fist.

'What's funny, Seamie?'

'Auntie Kitty buyin' me dis fer me birt'day.'

'Why? It's a nice present.'

'But she didn't used to be religious, not like us. She never used to go ta church, only fer weddin's and funerals, maybe at Christmas and Easter. After her and Tommy split up, she w's alw's at church.'

'Why do you think that was?'

'I dunno. Mam used to say folk turn to God when t'ings go bad.'

In the pitch blackness of the bog, a lightbulb went on in Una's head. It was a curious thing in Ireland, especially back then. All roads, good and bad, inevitably led to the church door.

CHAPTER 13

Una sat alone in the kitchen, stirring her tea and gazing at the whirlpool it created. A tea leaf had escaped from its teabag and it swirled around the circumference of the cup before gradually making its way to the centre where it spun furiously. The Church was at the centre. It was beginning to make sense to her now. Up until not so very long ago, the Church had been all-powerful in Ireland. Even the Irish government was under its thumb. Although the revelations and public scandals of late may have rubbed off some of the luster and left its reputation tarnished, the Church still wielded considerable influence in Ireland, especially among the older generation. She scooped out the tealeaf with her spoon, put it in the saucer and began talking to it.

What chance did she have against the likes of you? All that poor crathur had was her life and her virtue. First you took one and then you took the other and you left her in a stinking bog to rot. Did she love you I wonder? I suppose she must have if she was prepared to give up everything for you. Did you love her? I doubt it. Did you ask God for forgiveness? Perhaps you absolved yourself. Well you might have kept your reputation intact all these years but I swear to God I'll find out who you are and, whether you're dead or alive, I'll expose you. I'll get justice for that young woman if it kills me.

She picked up the tealeaf with a fingertip and wiped it away on her apron. What had started out as a mere diversion for Una had become a passionate quest for the truth.

*

Aine arrived home at eleven thirty and, much to Una's relief, she seemed to have put their run-in behind her. It was a trait of her granddaughter's that Una was particularly fond of. She could be spitting nails one minute, then forget about whatever it was and never mention it again. Like a passing squall, the lashing rain and gale force winds would soon give way to calm and sunshine.

'No telly again tonight, Nan?' She laughed. 'It's not broken is it?'

'No, pet,' said Una dreamily. 'I was just sitting here thinking.'

'Oh dear, that sounds ominous.' Aine's tone was cheerful. 'Did you catch that auld cat tonight.'

'I did as a matter of fact.' Una's tone was far from cheery and the smile slid from Aine's face. She sat down opposite her grandmother and leaned forward, her elbows resting on the table.

'And..?'

In measured tones Una told her what taken place, although she deliberately omitted to mention her own suspicions about the Church's involvement.

'Well!' said Aine. 'Well fair play to you, Nan! You must have enough there to justify re-opening the case, although I'm not sure whether Seamus would be considered a reliable witness.'

'You're to leave Seamie out of it,' Una told her.

'But without his testimony, we're no further forward.'

Una took her granddaughter's hand. 'Do you remember reading To Kill a Mockingbird?' she said. 'I gave you a copy years ago.'

'I do o'course, it made me want to become a lawyer. I wanted to fight for justice like Atticus Finch. Why?'

'Do you remember who the Mockingbird was?'

'Ah now it's been a long time since I read it.'

'I'll lend you my copy. Read it again with an adult's eyes.'

'So who was the Mockingbird and what's it got to do with this case?'

'It was Boo Radley, the gentle simpleton who kept himself to himself and wouldn't harm a fly. After he saved the children, Atticus and the sheriff decided that to make a hero of him, or to put him in the public eye, would be a sin. Like the hunter who kills a mockingbird for sport, it would be like killing innocence. Seamus is Boo Radley, do you see?'

'But there's no case without Seamus.'

'Give me a week, Aine. If I've hit a brick wall by then, you can do whatever you need to. You can tell Gerard everything but promise me, not a word to anyone until then.'

'I don't know, Nan, that's a big ask.'

'Just one week, that's all I'm asking. The poor girl has been buried for nearly seventy

years. One more week can't make much
difference.'

'Alright so, you have a week.'

Una was relieved. 'Grand,' she said. 'I'll go
and get you that book. Put the kettle on,
pet.'

*

Sunday came around and the three women
attended ten o'clock Mass. When they got
home, they began preparing for their dinner
guest. Joan worked her magic on the house
while grandmother and granddaughter
prepared dinner. Aine kept reminding Una
not to embarrass her in front of Gerard and
Una kept reminding Aine to keep what
she'd told her to herself. Finally they came
to an agreement; they would stop reminding
each other.

Una needn't have worried because not a
single word was mentioned at dinner about
the body found in the bog. Highly skilled
in the art of small talk, it was Joan's job to
orchestrate the conversation and in no time
she had the Inspector telling them about his
current case.

An elderly couple living in an isolated
cottage had been terrorised by two thugs
who'd followed them home from a

shopping trip. They'd been tied up with lamp cords and threatened with bodily harm. The thieves got away with thirty-one euro in cash and a bit of cheap jewellery but they'd left behind more fingerprints than you'd find in a school lunch room and had already been identified. Now all he had to do was throw a net over them. It wasn't a very exciting case to begin with but Joan insisted on knowing every last detail and, by the time he'd fleshed out the story, Una had lost the will to live. When the conversation finally flagged to the point where even Joan couldn't resuscitate it, Aine piped up.

'Have you ever read this, Gerard?' She held out her grandmother's dog-eared copy of To Kill a Mockingbird. Gerard took the book and looked at the back cover. He shook his head.

'I haven't,' he said, 'but I saw the film. Good story. Starred Gregory Peck as I remember.' He handed the book back to Aine and she put it on the table next to her plate.

'I read it in one sitting yesterday.' she said. Gerard waited for more but Aine just stared at the book. He wasn't quite sure whether or not to congratulate her and Joan was just about to step in when Aine spoke again.

'I don't think my future is with An Garda Síochána.' The announcement startled everyone at the table.

'What did you say?' Una thought her hearing must be going as well as her mind.

'I've been thinking about it for some time now, Nan.'

'But you've invested five years in the Force,' protested Gerard.

'Exactly, and what do I have to show for it? I've been stuck in a dead-end job ever since I left the Garda College. I've been overlooked for promotion twice and I just don't see a future in it for me.'

Gerard whistled between his teeth. 'That's a very big step to take, Aine, have you really thought it through? I mean, well the law is what you're trained for.'

'Then it'll come in handy when I'm taking my law degree.'

'You want to become a solicitor?' Gerard couldn't believe what he was hearing.

'Or a barrister, I don't know yet.'

'Can you afford it? Studying law isn't cheap you know.'

'I'll find a way.'

'Fair play to ya, girl!' blurted out Una. 'You finally came to your senses!'

Gerard felt suddenly maligned. 'Why? What's wrong with a career in law enforcement?'

'Nothing at all,' said Aine. 'It just isn't what I want to do any more.' Joan reached out and gently took her hand. 'I'm so pleased for you, my dear. You'll make an excellent job of it.' It seemed that Gerard was outnumbered.

'Well I think you're making a big mistake,' he said.

'Well it's just as well that I don't have to answer to you,' she retorted.

The atmosphere had become decidedly frosty around the table and, for the remainder of the meal, relations were strained between the two young people. Soon after dessert, the Inspector excused himself and left.

'Oh my goodness,' said Joan, smiling broadly, 'I didn't expect that today.'

Aine's eyes shone bright. 'No wedding bells for me anytime soon.' She grinned. 'How do you feel about that, Nan?'

'Ah, pet.' Una threw her arms around her granddaughter. 'I'm so proud of you.'

CHAPTER 14

'I wish that poor girl didn't have to work on Sundays.' Joan dried the dishes as Una washed them. Aine had gone upstairs to change for work.

'Will we get the criminals to take the weekends off?' laughed Una.

'You know, if we're going to be asking questions at the church, we're going to have to think of a plausible reason why we're doing it.'

'Hauld yer whisht!' Una pressed a rubber-gloved finger to her lips. 'Aine doesn't know I suspect the Church's involvement. We'll talk about it when she's gone.' Joan nodded. Just then Aine came bounding down the stairs. She looked at the kitchen clock.

'Jesus, look at the time, I'm late! Bye, Joan. See you later, Nan.' The back door slammed behind her and Joan stared at it for a moment.

'Young people,' she said, shaking her head, 'always in a hurry. She'll be furious you know when she finds out you've been keeping information from her.'

'No doubt, Joan, but I'll have to cross that bridge when I come to it.'

'So, what's the plan?'

'Well that's why I wanted to talk to you. C'mere, sit down, I'll make us a cuppa.' Una put the kettle on while Joan made herself comfortable at the table. 'If we go to Father Nolan and just come out with it, he'll be on the defensive straight away. We're going to have to think of a flanking manoeuvre, a roundabout way of getting the information we want.'

'I see,' replied Joan, 'yes.' She sat in silent thought for a few minutes before exclaiming, 'Bridie O'Brien!'

'The sacristan? What about her?'

'She's the perfect person to ask. Apart from Father Nolan, Bridget's closer to the Church than anyone in Ballyanny... and she soaks up gossip like a mop. If anyone knows anything, it's Bridie.'

'But she'd be a child when Kitty disappeared, five or six at the most. Anyway, Bridie's only been sacristan for the last forty years or so. The information we're after goes back seventy years.'

'Hmmm, let me think,' contemplated Joan. 'I'm just trying to remember who was sacristan before Bridie.'

'I can see her face,' said Una, narrowing her eyes, 'but I can't remember her name. Jayzus, she was a miserable-looking woman, and a disposition to match if I remember right. Antisocial isn't in it, she barely left her house unless it was to do her church duties. God, what was her name? Began with a C.'

'Concepta!' declared Joan triumphantly. 'Concepta Regan!'

'That's it! Good woman! No wonder the poor soul was miserable with a name like that.'

'I rather like it,' replied Joan. 'It's unusual, like Beyonce or Madonna.'

'You would,' scoffed Una. 'Whatever happened to her?'

'Madonna? Oh, I think she's living in.....'

'Concepta!'

'Oh yes, of course. Well she had dreadful arthritis you know. The poor woman was in constant pain. Her hands were all twisted up in the end. By the time she gave up her duties, she was walking on two sticks. Goodness only knows how she managed to work as long as she did.'

'She's still alive, isn't she?'

'I haven't the slightest idea.'

'Well we'll talk to Bridie first. How do you think we should approach her without making her suspicious.'

'I've been thinking about that, my dear. As you know, I'm a published writer and....'

'I'm not sure that having a few letters published in the Irish Times qualifies you as an author, Joan.'

'I didn't say I was an author.' Indignation wasn't considered ladylike in Joan's world so hers was barely perceptible. 'The Irish Times is a publication and they printed my letters.'

'Go on, I'll let you off so.'

'We'll tell Bridie that I'm writing a history of the parish with a feature on the daily running of the church. We'll say people would be interested to learn about the duties and responsibilities of a sacristan. We'll tell her it's for the parish magazine.'

'Good thinking, Joan, appeal to her ego.'

'We all have one,' said Joan, smiling.

'I didn't know you could be so devious,' replied Una, smiling too.

'I was taught by a professional. Don't forget my Thomas was a solicitor.'

'We'll take a notebook with us, make it look like a proper interview.'

'No need, my dear, I have a little voice recorder that I use to compile my shopping lists.'

'Now she tells me! I wish I'd known that when I was going to talk to Seamus.'

'Well that's what you get for keeping secrets from me.'

'You're right, pet. I should have told you sooner.' She held out her hand. 'No more secrets, promise. We're in this together from now on, agreed?'

'Partners,' said Joan with a firm shake of her friend's hand.

*

Aine slept in the following morning. She had a run of night shifts ahead of her and sleep was a rare commodity that must be well spent. Una left her a note on the kitchen table before going over the road. As they sat in Joan's kitchen drinking tea, Joan made a suggestion.

'I think perhaps I should conduct the interview,' she said, worried that she might hurt her friend's feelings. 'I love you dearly but you can be as blunt as a cricket ball sometimes.' Una was well aware of her shortcomings. She knew that subtlety wasn't her strong suit but still, it stung coming from her best friend.

'I can be discrete,' she protested.

'I know you can, my dear, but we only get one chance at this.' Una knew she was right. It was true that she had a tendency to be brusque, whereas Joan was skilled in the art of rhetoric as well as the art of diplomacy.

'Where will you hide the recording device?'

'I've got it right here.' Joan pulled out of her blouse pocket what looked to Una like a fat pen. 'I've had it on 'record' ever since you arrived.'

'You have? Play it back, let me hear it.' Joan did as instructed. 'Jesus!' exclaimed Una. 'Do I really sound like that?'

Joan laughed. 'Yes, dear, you do.'

'Well thank God it won't be me doing the talking. I sound like a goose! Your voice is like a lark singing compared to my gruff tone.'

The two ladies finished their tea and Joan washed up. She never left dirty dishes to come back to. Together they walked the short distance to St. Brendan's Church and, as luck would have it, Bridie was outside sweeping the front steps. She looked up as they approached. It was Joan who spoke first.

The Bog Body

'Good morning, Bridie, lovely day.'

'Grand day altogether, Joan. How're ya keeping Una?' It was an Irish salutation rather than a question and didn't require an answer. 'If it's Fadder Nolan ye're after, he's gone fishin' wit' George Webber. I'm glad to have him out from under me feet.'

'Actually, Bridie, it was you we wanted to talk to.'

'Me? What would ye be wanting wit' me?'

'Well I'm writing an article for the parish magazine, my dear, and I wanted to highlight the day-to-day duties of St. Brendan's sacristan. The congregation don't realise all the hard work you do and I thought it was about time someone sang your praises.' *She's good*, thought Una, *I'll give her that.*

'Ah sure it's just like keepin' a big house,' said Bridie, 'only o'course it's Gods house, so I'm glad to do it.'

'You're too modest, Bridget, I'm sure there's more to it than that. How long have you been sacristan now?'

'Nineteen seventy-seven I started.'

'Really? As long ago as that! Aren't you great. And who was the priest back then?'

'Ah that would be Father Hogan. Lovely fella, terrible problem with wind though.

The man could fart fer Ireland. Don't be writin' that now!'

Joan smiled. 'I won't. And who did you take over from? Who was sacristan before you?'

'Ah, the witch!' declared Bridget. 'Sister Concepta. Well, she was a nun when she first came, just after the war. She was a Sister of Mercy but she gave up her habit and vows a couple o' years later. What an aul' bitch she was! Thought everyone was going to hell but her and the priest.'

'What priest was that?'

'Now she served under Fadder Delaney, Francis his first name was. Ah Jayzus, a more handsome man you never saw. Could have been a film star with all that jet black, curly hair and them blue eyes. He was a Dubliner, came from a rich family. Big strappin' lad, all the women loved him. The men liked him too. Sure everybody liked him but he only stayed a few years. Upped and left suddenly. He went to Rome and was made a bishop in the end. Finished up in America... Milwaukee, Illinois if I remember right.'

'Is Father Delaney still alive, Bridget?'

'God no, he's been dead a long time.'

'And what happened to Concepta?'

'Well she was in Sacred Heart... you know, the Nursing Home in Killenaule. I didn't hear a death notice read out for her on Tipp FM so she must still be alive. She has to be well into her nineties by now.'

Una spoke for the first time. 'What can you tell us about Kitty Egan?' Bridget jumped as if she'd been jabbed with a cattle prod.

'Never heard of her,' she said abruptly,' and I'm busy. I don't have time fer dis.' She turned her back on them and resumed her sweeping with vigour. The two friends stood in silence for a moment, then walked away. Una took her friend's arm and leaned into her.

'I think we hit a nerve there,' she whispered.

CHAPTER 15

The two friends sat in Joan's kitchen drinking tea and eating scones. Joan dabbed at her mouth with a napkin.

'I thought that went quite well, dear, don't you?'

'Until I opened my big gob,' replied Una through a mouthful of scone.

'Oh don't worry about that. We'd already got the information we were looking for.'

'Yes but now she'll be wondering what we're up to. I'll bet my last teabag she's already called Father Nolan.'

'Let her, what harm can it do?' Joan flipped through a telephone directory she kept in a kitchen drawer. 'Now let's see, what's the number of that nursing facilty in Killenaule?'

'What if Concepta doesn't receive visitors?'

'Then we'll have to get in some other way, come up with a ruse of some kind.'

'Will we wear false beards?' Una grinned. 'Pretend we're plumbers?'

'Can you see me in a pair of tradesmen's overalls?' They laughed as Joan dialled the number. A receptionist answered with her well-practiced monologue.

'Sacred Heart Nursing Home, this is Marie speaking, how may I help you?'

'Ah yes, hello. I'm enquiring to see if you have a Concepta Regan in residence?'

'Who's calling please?'

'It's a friend.'

'A friend? Jayzus, that's a good one! I didn't think she had any.' Beyond the affected greeting with which she answered the phone, Marie's South Tipp accent was as thick as they came. Joan raised her eyebrows in Una's direction and put her hand over the mouthpiece.

'You have to hear this,' she whispered, putting the phone on speaker.

'We weren't really close friends,' Joan told her. 'More acquaintances really. I knew Concepta when she was sacristan at Saint Brendan's. Is she well?'

'Physically, she's as well as a ninety-t'ree year-old with rheumatoid art'ritis can be.'

'How long have you had her with you now?'

'Longer than I've been here anyway, longer than any of the staff, twenty years at least.'

'I see, and tell me, does Concepta entertain visitors?' Marie erupted into laughter.

'I wouldn't know, she's never had any, but I'm sure she'd entertain 'em.'

'I'm sorry. I don't follow.'

The receptionist lowered her voice to the point where it was barely audible. 'Between you and me, yer wan is as mad as a box of frogs. The girls flip a coin to decide who'll take her meals or change her bedlinen, or bathe her.'

'Is she coherent?'

'Sometimes. She's been tested for Dementia but it's not that. Her doctor t'inks she's delusional. He's tried to get her admitted to a psychiatric facility but the paperwork always seems to go astray. It's a mystery. We can't even get her a psychiatric consultation.'

'Oh dear, the poor woman. Does she mix with the other residents?'

'God no. She stays in her room all day praying, but it's just as well. She calls all us women sluts and hoors and harlots and all the men fornicators. She won't answer you unless you call her Sister Concepta and she hardly eats enough to keep body and soul together. She constantly bangs on about some priest from the past and reckons everyone else will burn in hell. Listen, I've said too much. I'll lose me job if they find out I've been talking about her.'

'Don't worry, Marie, and thank you for your candour. Bye now, bye bye, thank you, byebyebyebye.' Joan hung up and the two women looked at each other. Una was the first to speak.

'Put the kettle on, pet, this is a two-cup dilemma.'

'It's certainly going to require some thought,' said Joan as she filled the kettle with water.

'Delusional, the girl said. I wonder if her delusions are just fantasy or whether they're memories. We have to talk to her, Joan.'

'Ideally, yes, but I don't relish the thought of driving all the way to Killenaule just to be called a whore.'

'What if we dressed the part?'

'Dressed like whores?' Joan was outraged. 'I don't think so!'

'No.' Una grinned at the thought of Joan in high heels and a short skirt. 'She's unlikely to call us hoors if we dress as nuns. It'll be gas, like playing dress up when we were kids.'

'Whenever I dressed up as a child, I was always a princess.'

'Well, your highness, we'd better go shopping for material.'

Joan sighed. 'And I'd better get out my sewing machine.'

*

When Una got home, she found Aine standing in the kitchen looking out at the back garden. She seemed lost in thought.

'Wanna cup, pet?' asked Una, taking her apron off a peg by the door.

Aine nearly jumped out of her skin. 'God!' she exclaimed, clapping her hand to her chest. 'You scared the bejusus outta me. I didn't hear you come in.'

'What's up?'

'Gerard just phoned.'

'To apologise was it?'

'Apologise? Why would he apologise? No, something strange happened when he got to his office this morning.'

'Strange how?'

'There was an envelope on his desk.'

'What's strange about that?'

'It had photographs inside. Photographs of him leaving our house on Thursday, and again yesterday.'

'What in God's name....?'

'There was a note with them, it just had one word on it.'

'What did it say?'

'Fraternisation.'

'Frat....? Sure he was only having dinner with us. I invited him and he came. What's the big deal?'

'Superiors and subordinates aren't supposed to socialise privately after hours.'

'Ah, that's ridiculous.'

'It's policy.

'But who on God's earth would go to the trouble of lurking outside to take photos?'

'I don't know. Neither does he.'

'This has something to do with that woman in the bog, doesn't it.'

'It's a warning, that's for sure, but we're not jumping to any conclusions about the reason for it. The fact is, he could get into trouble and so could I.'

'Ah I'm sorry, pet. I had no idea I was violating some daft rule.'

'It's not your fault, Nan, but one thing's for sure. Detective Inspector Quinn won't be coming to dinner again anytime soon. I'm afraid your career as a matchmaker is over before it began. Now where's my laptop? I need to download an application form and syllabus for my law degree.'

'That's the spirit! When one door closes, another one opens.'

'Or the one that's closing knocks you on your arse.'

CHAPTER 16

That afternoon, the two friends headed for Urlingford in Joan's old but immaculately-kept Nissan Micra. She was a careful driver, Una might have said slow.

'Could you pick it up a little, pet? I'm getting old here.'

'I'm adhering to the speed limit,' Joan protested. Una leaned over and peered at the speedometer.

'You're 10 kilometers under the speed limit.'

'One can't be too careful on these narrow country lanes. One never knows what's around the bend.'

'One could put one's foot down just a tad,' mocked Una. 'At our age, we need to get where we're going before we forget where we're going.'

'Concepta has been in that nursing home over twenty years. A day or two more won't hurt.'

'It's not Concepta I'm worried about. I need the loo... and soon!'

'Why didn't you go before we left?'

'Because I didn't need to go then!'

'Weak bladder,' said Joan, nodding sagely. 'There are exercises for that.'

'There's nothing wrong with my bladder, thank you. I drank enough tea to sink the Titanic, and these pot holes in the road aren't helping.'

'Relax and enjoy the scenery, we'll get there when we get there.'

'We'll get there with a wet passenger seat if you don't get a move on, and why do you keep looking in the rear view mirror?'

'We've had a big black car behind us ever since we left the village.'

'Here, pull over in the entrance to that field. I can't hold it any longer, I'll go behind the hedge, and whoever's in the car can get past.' Joan complied and Una leapt out when the car came to a halt. Before ducking behind the hedge, she waited for the black car to pass. It drove slowly past them and Una tried to get a look at the driver but the windows were too dark. Once past, it accelerated away with a roar.

'Did you see the driver of that car?' she asked Joan when she got back in.

'No, I didn't look. Why?'

The Bog Body

'Never mind. I think I'm paranoid.'

In under ten minutes, they had arrived in Urlingford. The small town was on the border between Tipperary and Kilkenny, its long main street lined with shops and pubs. To the more sophisticated visitor, it might not have looked like much and it's true that, like most Irish market towns, Urlingford's glory days had long since gone. Too many shops were vacant, the paint peeling from their signs, and few residents could find work locally. They had to commute to larger towns... Kilkenny, Cork, even Limerick.

Nostalgia was not a sentiment enjoyed by most of the Irish in Ireland. Emigrants took that with them when they left long ago and it lives on today in their descendants. For those who went, absence made the heart grow fonder, or at least it blunted the memory, whereas as here, reminders of how it was were everywhere and the old days were still too fresh in people's minds to regard them as good old days.

Joan parallel parked her Micra behind a John Deere tractor outside the Urlingford Arms. The Arms was somewhat of a landmark and, in the days before motorways, it had marked the half way point between Dublin and Cork. As well as a hotel, it was a pub and restaurant and, over the years, had become a popular lunchtime meeting place for the older residents of the town. No-nonsense meals were served up by the same waitresses who'd been serving them for years, to old friends who discussed the latest deaths and traded local gossip over a pint of the black stuff.

Una had her eyes on the ground, trying not to trip on the cracked pavement, when she almost bumped into Joan as her friend stopped abruptly.

'Here we are,' announced Joan, 'Martha's Fabrics.'

The shop frontage was tiny, no more than ten feet across, barely wide enough for a door and a small window. Joan tried the door handle but it wouldn't budge. She shielded her eyes against the glass. 'There's a light on,' she said, 'she must be open.' She tapped at the glass and a frail voice crackled from within.

'Alright, alright, hold yer horses, I'm coming.'

They heard a bolt slide across and the door opened. A toothless woman stood inside, squinting at them. She was stooped with age and the skin on her face was as creased and puckered as the blue paint on her door.

She studied Joan's face for a moment, searching her memory for a name.

'Joan, is it? Joan Cahill? Well, well, I haven't seen you in donkey's years.' Joan greeted her as only Joan could. She gently took the old woman's shrivelled hands and kissed each wrinkled cheek.

'Hello, Martha, dear. How have you been?'

'Ah sure not too bad,' she rasped. 'Come in, come in, we're lettin' all the heat out.' The temperature inside the shop was stiflingly hot and a musty smell pervaded the room, a combination of damp, turf burning in the stove and cloth that had been on the shelves too long. Una unbuttoned her cardigan and the ancient woman turned to her.

'And who's this?'

Joan made the introductions and Martha asked the standard rhetorical question. 'Will ye have tay?' A kettle on the stove already had steam rising from its spout and the old woman measured out four spoons of loose tea into a teapot, one each and one for the pot, before pouring in the boiling water. Una looked around the shop and thought it looked more like a museum than a haberdashery, the main item on display an ancient Singer sewing machine which stood beside a big brown counter. It was as if, when they had stepped over the threshold, they'd stepped back in time to the 1950s, maybe even as far back as the 1930s.

'How's business?' asked Joan.

'Ah, sure no one makes their own dresses anymore,' lamented the old woman as she poured tea into three cracked and mismatched cups. 'Nobody sews even, they don't have the time fer it. Sure clothes are disposable nowadays. Everything's made in China out of cheap shite and when it wears out after a couple of washes, they just buy more cheap shite. They bring shtuff in fer me to alter alright, then they complain about the price. Ah sure don't listen to me, I'm ranting. What is it ye're after today? I've a lovely roll of Donegal tweed, new in last year.'

'We're making costumes for a fancy dress party, Martha,' said Joan, trying to avoid eye contact with Una. 'My friend and I are going dressed as nuns.'

The old woman cackled, 'Well now, that would have been frowned on in my day but times change. Did you have any particular order in mind?'

'Sisters of Mercy,' Una blurted. Martha scanned the shelves and stroked the dozen or so long, grey hairs on her chin.

The Bog Body

'I have plenty of brown. You could be Franciscan, or Carmelite.'

'Sisters of Mercy,' repeated Una.

'Grand so, that's robin's egg blue.' She took down a roll of blue material and looked both women up and down. 'T'ree yards fer you, Joan.' She looked at Una again. 'Four fer you, missus.' Una sniffed. 'And I'll t'row in a few yards of white fer free.'

The old woman expertly measured out and cut the material, then she folded it carefully and wrapped it in brown paper.

'Twenty euro,' she said, 'the lot.'

'That's cheap!' Una couldn't help herself. Joan dug her in the ribs.

'If I don't get rid of all the shtuff on these shelves, they'll be using it to wrap me in when I die. If ya want I'll make them up fer yous. Twenty euro apiece.' Joan scooped up the package.

'Thanks anyway, Martha, I'm doing it myself.'

As they were heading out the door they heard, 'Five apiece. I'll do both fer ten euro. I got nutt'n better to do.' They froze in the doorway and looked at each other. Una turned to the old seamstress.

'Can you have them ready by noon tomorrow?'

'I can o'course.'

'Excellent,' said Joan, handing the parcel back to the old woman. 'Thank you, Martha, we'll be back for them tomorrow.'

'Do ya still make yer lemon drizzle cake?'

Joan laughed. 'I'll bring you some, see you tomorrow at twelve.' The two friends walked out into the crisp, early Autumn air.

'Do we need anything else while we're in town?' Joan asked.

'I was thinking, we should take something for Concepta. If she's as miserable an old bat as they say, a gift might make her more amiable. We'll call it a peace offering.'

'Hahaa! Beware of Greeks bearing gifts!'

'And be very afraid of two old Irish women bearing gifts!'

'I'd prefer senior, thank you. And I'm not Irish, I'm English.'

'You were married to an Irishman.'

'So?'

'That makes you Irish by injection.'

'Really, Una, you can be so vulgar.'

Una ignored her friend's rebuke. 'Vincent's is only four doors down, we're bound to find something in there.'

In no time at all they were inside the St. Vincent de Paul charity shop. A radio was tuned to Tipp FM and Trudi Lalor's country music show was playing. While Joan made a beeline for a shelf that groaned under the weight of cups, saucers and glassware, Una headed for a counter with a middle-aged man sitting behind it. He seemed lost in the voice that came from the radio and, as she approached, he held up a finger causing her to pause.

'Gorgeous speaking voice, hasn't she?' Trudi Lalor was Una's favourite radio presenter too so she agreed, but she was on a mission.

'Rosary beads,' she whispered, not wishing to interrupt his listening pleasure. Without getting up off his seat, he produced a large cardboard box from underneath the counter and put it on top.

'Help yourself,' he said. 'We get lots in when the old folk die. Not much call for 'em these days.' He lost himself again in the fantasy he'd been acting out with the faceless voice coming from the radio, leaving Una to root through dozens of rosary beads. Almost immediately she found a set of large beads, the kind that nuns wore.

'I'll take these,' she said, more to herself than to the disinterested volunteer. She put them on the counter and delved back into the box, trying to untangle the beads as she went deeper. There were wooden ones, fake pearl ones, glass ones and ones made from just about anything that could be formed into the shape of a bead. Most were broken, some had half the beads missing. She was looking for a second set of large beads and she finally spotted one coiled like a snake near the bottom.

'Gotcha!' She grabbed them and hauled them out. She set them down on the counter with the others and went back in. A glint of olive green had caught her eye and she plunged her hand down through the beads. 'Please don't be broken,' she said under her breath. She pulled out the rosary and untangled it. It was a pretty Connemara marble set and it looked quite old. 'I should keep you for myself,' she said as she held it up to the light. The craftsmanship on the crucifix told her it wasn't a cheap knockoff. 'You look like a peace offering if ever I saw one,' she said, then raised her voice.

'How much?'

'What's that? Oh, I don't know. A euro each.' Una took the coins out of her purse and slapped them down on the counter. She put the beads into her handbag, then leaned over the counter and nodded in the direction of the radio.

'She'd eat you fer breakfast,' she said, 'then spit you out.'

'Ah but what a way to go, missus,' he grinned. 'What a way to go.'

Una wandered over to where Joan was picking up cups and saucers and checking them for hallmarks.

'Ready, pet?'

'We only just got here.'

'We've been in here over half an hour. I want to get home before Aine goes to work.'

Joan picked up one more saucer and turned it over, then put it down and followed her friend out of the shop.

CHAPTER 17

Aine was getting ready to leave for work when the two friends arrived home.

'Well,' she said. On its own, the word was used liberally throughout Tipperary to mean hello, how are you, what's happening, or a combination of all three.

'I'm glad we caught you, pet,' said Una, 'we've been in Urlingford.'

'Ah right. See anything interesting?'

'Not really. We just had a wander around, bumped into an old friend of Joan's.'

'Oh that reminds me, Joan' said Aine, 'do you know someone with a black Mercedes, a new one, one of those big C-Class jobs?'

Joan laughed. 'No, I wish I did. Why do you ask?'

'One was parked outside your house earlier, it sat with the engine running for ages. I went out in the end to see if I could help whoever it was, but they took off before I could even get a look at the number plate.'

'Did you see the driver?' asked Una.

Aine shook her head. 'It had those blacked-out windows.'

'Goodness, Una!' exclaimed Joan. 'Do you think it's the same one that followed us?'

Aine turned to her grandmother. 'I thought you didn't see anything interesting.'

'Ah sure that was nothing.' The lie was unconvincing. 'A big black car was behind us, that's all.'

'Where was this?'

Una waved her hand in the general direction. 'Up by the entrance to Kilcooley. It's no big deal, it soon passed us out when we stopped for me to have a wee behind the hedge.'

'Honestly, Nan, I've told you before, there are exercises you can do for that weak bladder of yours. Did the car pass you straight away?'

'There's nothing wrong with my waterworks, thank you! It slowed down as it passed us, but then it carried on.'

'Nan...' Una knew exactly what her granddaughter's anxious expression conveyed.

'Stop worrying, and don't forget, I still have five more days left.'

'You could be in danger. I don't like it.'

'Sure if someone was following us, they'd hardly use a big fancy Merc now would they? That would be far too conspicuous around here. I told you, stop worrying.'

'I think we should tell Aine what we know, dear,' said Joan. Una gave her a withering look.

Aine addressed the weakest link. 'Good idea, Joan. Why don't you tell me?'

'Hauld yer whisht, Joanie! We don't want the shades all over this messing it up before we can find out the truth.'

'The shades?' Aine looked at her grandmother in disbelief. 'What are you, a gangster?'

'There's a cover up,' blurted Joan. Una threw her hands up in frustration. 'And the police are involved somehow,' added Joan meekly.

'I'd already worked that out for myself, but who's behind it? Do you know?'

Una realised she had to give her granddaughter something. 'It's the Church,' she said resignedly.

'And how did you two ageing amateur sleuths manage to come to that conclusion?'

'You told us.'

'What's that supposed to mean?'

'You told us that most cold cases get solved by old secrets coming out.'

The Bog Body

'I don't suppose you have any proof to back up this theory of yours?'

'No, but what I do have are five more days to get to the bottom of it.'

Aine knew she'd get no more out of her grandmother and she was late for work so she left. 'Just be careful!' she shouted before she slammed the door behind her.

The two friends spent the evening transcribing all the events that had occurred since the body was discovered in the bog.

'We need to document everything,' Una told Joan, 'before we forget the details.'

'The problem is, it's all circumstantial,' said Joan. 'None of this would stand up in a court of law.'

'Listen, we've ruffled a few feathers. Let's see what comes out of that and, anyway, I'd say it's the court of public opinion that's of more importance here than a court of law.

*

Next morning, the two women planned their strategy.

'We'll go the long way to Urlingford,' Una told Joan. 'We'll drive through Clonimiclon, then on to Grange. We'll head out towards Kilkenny and come into Urlingford from the opposite direction.'

'Do you think that will keep whoever it is off our tail?'

'Probably not, but at least it's scenic. Wait! On second thoughts, I have a better idea. You go in your car and I'll go in mine. That's it! We'll head in different directions. I'll leave at half eleven and go through Clonimiclon. You wait fifteen minutes and drive the usual route.'

Joan giggled excitedly. 'You have a real knack for subterfuge, Mrs. Murphy,' she said. 'You should have been a spy.'

'The name's Bond,' grinned Una. 'Jane Bond.'

It was eleven thirty when Una set out on her circuitous journey. She spent as much time looking in the rear view mirror as she did watching where she was going but, by the time Clonimiclon was behind her, she realised the mouse wasn't nibbling the cheese. She stopped at the side of the road and tried to ring Joan on her mobile but couldn't get a signal. Alright, so, she said to herself, we'll wing it and see who makes a mistake first. She turned her car around in the narrow lane and headed back towards Gortnahoe. She glanced at her watch and realised she wouldn't make it to Urlingford in time for her rendezvous with Joan. She pulled over and tried the phone again. This time she got a signal.

'Where are you?' Joan sounded nervous.

'I'm a few minutes away. What's the matter?'

'That black car! It's already here! It passed me out before I got into town and it's parked outside the Urlingford Arms.'

'Is the driver still in it?'

'No! I don't know! Una, I'm frightened.'

'Calm down, Joan, just stick to the plan. Go to Martha's, I'll meet you in there. I'll only be a few minutes.'

Una slowed to a crawl as she entered the town. Just as Joan had said, the shiny black Mercedes was parked outside the Arms, directly behind the same John Deere that hadn't moved a millimeter since yesterday. *Alright, mister smarty-pants*, she thought, *you're not so clever after all*. She pulled her ageing Ford Fiesta to within inches of the big car's rear bumper and pulled on her emergency brake as hard as she could. *You're going nowhere*.

She leapt out of the car and hurried to the dress shop. She opened the door but didn't go in.

'Joan!' she hissed. 'Come on, quick!'

They hurried to Joan's car. They'd planned it so she would park facing Killenaule for a quick getaway. As they drove past the Urlingford Arms, a tall man in a long black overcoat was coming out. He threw his hands in the air when he saw his Mercedes blocked in and looked up to see their car sailing past.

Joan sped out of town at a surprising speed. 'Where will we get changed?' she asked, her voice quivering. 'Will we go home?'

'No! Head straight for Killenaule. We'll stop at Perry's in Ballynonty on the way.'

'I'm not cut out for this, Una.' Joan was still shaken. 'This whole business has me completely unnerved.'

'Pull yourself together, Joanie. Everything's going to plan.'

It started to rain and Joan switched on the wipers. She found their monotonous click-clack almost calming but, even so, she kept checking the rearview mirror, expecting to see the big black car bearing down on them.

'Stop worrying,' her friend told her. 'The only way he's getting out of there is to have my car towed away, or the tractor. That'll take at least a couple of hours with this rain and, even then, he doesn't know where we're headed.'

'He seems to know more than you're giving him credit for.'

'We're always one step ahead, Joan. He's just following, that's all.'

'They used the restroom at Perry's to change into their nuns' habits. Unsurprisingly, it took Joan longer.

'Here,' said Una, handing her one of the larger sets of rosary beads. 'You need to hang this on your belt, like so.' She gestured to the set hanging from her own belt.

'I know how nuns dress!' Joan said, her tone slightly petulant. 'I did go to a convent school you know.'

'Relax, Joan, take a deep breath. You're wound as tight as a spool of thread.'

'I can't help it. You would be too if you'd had a mad man chasing you!'

'I doubt if he's mad, not in that sense anyway. I'll bet he's furious that I boxed his car in though.'

'I have to say, that was very clever of you.'

'A spur of the moment thing, Joanie. Opportunity knocked and I answered. Now listen, we've got one shot at this so let's get ourselves together. Where's the voice recorder?' Joan patted her collar.

*

Two elderly nuns in a Nissan Micra drove slowly up the winding driveway of Killenaule's Sacred Heart Nursing Home. They parked around the back.

'Is it switched on?' asked Una. Joan reached under her scapular for a moment, then nodded. 'Good. Well, here goes nothing.'

They walked around to the front and rang the bell. The door was half-glazed and it was only a few seconds before they saw a slightly confused receptionist coming to answer it. Before the girl could gather her senses, Joan spoke.

'We're here to see Concepta. I talked to someone yesterday on the phone.'

'Errr... that was me,' stammered the bewildered receptionist. 'I'm sorry, Sister, I think I spoke out of turn.'

Joan played her part well. She held the young woman's hand and spoke comfortingly. 'Not at all, my dear. I'm sure Concepta would try the patience of a saint.'

'Did you speak to someone after you rang, Sister?

'I don't follow, child.'

'It's just that Concepta is being transferred to a psychiatric facility tomorrow morning. I thought perhaps you'd spoken to someone.'

'What a remarkable coincidence!' Joan smiled sweetly, then glanced at Una.

'Good job,' mumbled Una. Marie turned her attention to the plump nun now.

'I'm sorry, Sister, what was that?' she said.

'May we see her?' said Una.

'Oh, I'm sorry! You can o'course. She's in a front room on the first floor. I'll take you there.'

CHAPTER 18

The building itself was impressive. Neo-Gothic in style, it had been purposely built as a parochial house for clergy serving at the adjacent parish church and its austere, grey facade belied the interior. They were taken through an antechamber which served as a waiting room, past a reception desk and into a cavernous entrance hall that rose two stories high. A grand staircase swept up from the centre to the top floor where ornately-carved plaster mouldings on the ceiling added to the building's period character. Far from being a sterile world of white-walled corridors and swinging double doors, this place had more of a museum quality about it. Instead of displaying objects of antiquity, it was the final dignified repose of those living out their last days on earth.

A musty odour mingled with the smell of disinfectant and three ancient people sat on benches. None of them noticed the newcomers.

The Bog Body

A tiny old woman sat gazing at the door they'd just come through and rocked, waiting for a visitor who might never come. Her companions were two men whose chins rested on their chests as they slept peacefully, dreaming of lives lived long ago.

The receptionist spoke in hushed tones. 'They've just finished their lunch,' she explained, 'so it's quiet. Normally, visitors see the residents in our day room, there's a nice turf fire in there, but we have to make an exception for Concepta. If we try to get her out of her room, she becomes... let's say disruptive. Follow me.' She started up the staircase. 'Mind yourselves on the steps now.'

They ascended the stairs in almost reverent silence. When they reached the top Marie led them to one of the doors off the wide landing. 'I'll introduce you,' she told them, 'but then I have to get back to reception. Remember to address her as Sister.' She tapped on the door and walked in.

The room was sparsely furnished. A set of dentures smiled at them from a glass tumbler on the bedside table, and a pine air freshener only partially masked the smell of urine. The magnolia-painted walls were bare, except for a crucifix opposite the bed and a picture of the Blessed Virgin Mary above a boarded-up fireplace.

An old woman lay propped up in bed, the sheets tucked neatly around her. She looked painfully thin and frail. Her eyes were sunken deep into their sockets and her nose was hooked down. Her lips were folded into her toothless mouth and dried spittle stained her chin.

'What do you want, you hoor?' she spat at Marie. 'Can't you see I'm praying?' The young girl was accustomed to the old woman and didn't seem to notice what she'd said.

'I have visitors for you, Sister Concepta.'

'If it's that feckin' dentist and his harlot, tell him the teeth don't fit!' A thin stream of saliva dribbled down her chin.

'It's not the dentist, Sister, he said he won't be coming back. Sister Joan and Sister Una are here to see you.'

'Well go on, then! Feck off and leave us alone. And don't listen at the door, you daughter of Babylon!' Marie left the room and Joan addressed the old woman.

'Good afternoon, Sister Concepta,' she said, 'I'm Sister Joan.' She held out her hand but the woman didn't take it so Joan motioned towards Una. 'And this is Sister Una.'

'Where in God's name have ye been? I've been here at least three weeks, I thought ye'd forgotten me. Have ye come to take me home? This place is like a whorehouse, people sneaking in and out at all times of the day and night. They try and touch me you know!'

Una knew she couldn't be trusted to conduct the interview so she deferred to Joan. 'She's all yours,' she said under her breath.

'What did she say?' snarled Concepta.

Joan thought fast. 'Sister Una reminded me that we brought you a present from Lourdes.'

'What? What did you bring me?' The old woman's eyes lit up as Joan took out a green-beaded rosary from her pocket and laid it on the bed.

'We got these in Lourdes,' she told her. Concepta picked them up and inspected them.

'No you didn't,' she snarled. 'You're lying! These are Irish beads.' It had of course been a lie but nothing like the whopper that Joan was about to tell.

'You're right,' she said, 'they are, and an old Irish friend of yours told us to give them to you.'

'What friend?'

'Bishop Delaney from Milwaukee in America. Francis Delaney.'

'Frankie?' The old woman's harsh expression relaxed. Her face softened and her pale blue eyes watered up. 'You saw my Frankie?' She struggled to haul herself up into a sitting position. 'How is he?'

'He's as well as can be expected,' said Joan. *As well as can be expected for someone who's been dead for years*, she thought.

'Didn't you think him handsome?' Concepta looked from one to the other but she wasn't seeking confirmation.

'He's the most handsome man I ever saw,' she said, her gaze wandering to the crucifix on the wall. She stared at it, unseeing, as her mind travelled back in time to a young priest with a mop of curly black hair and blue eyes. 'All the women wanted him, you know. They were all hoors and harlots, the lot of them, temptresses sent by Satan to debauch him with their painted lips and their worldly ways.' Her voice was full of hatred again now and she was in danger of working herself into a frenzy.

The Bog Body

'Were you in love with him?' asked Una. It was blunt but someone had to get the ball rolling. The old woman flashed her a look of disdain.

'What would you know about it? Mine wasn't a love of the flesh, it was spiritual. Frankie was my Anam Cara. His soul spoke to mine. I knew what was best for him.'

'He spoke very fondly of you,' offered Una.

'Did he?' The old woman's eyes were almost pleading. 'What did he say?'

Una decided to chance her arm. 'He told us you'd saved him from a crisis of faith.'

'I'd have done anything for him. I didn't just save him from a crisis of faith, I saved him from eternal damnation!' *Now we're getting somewhere*, thought Una. She decided to chance the other arm.

'Are you talking about Kathleen Egan?' The old crone's eyes flashed at the sound of the name. She set her mouth in a thin line.

'Don't mention her to me! That miserable defiled pot of flesh thought my Frankie was going to run off with her, but I showed her. I fixed it.'

'Did you put the stocking around her neck?'

'He told you about that?'

'I know about it.'

'I had it in my hand when she knocked on the door. It was late at night. I was doing my laundry. The little bitch just stood there with a stupid smile on her face and a suitcase in her hand. It was the smile of the devil. She WAS the devil. He was mocking me, telling me he'd won. I had to stop him. I threw the stocking around her neck but before I could throttle her she stepped back and fell down the steps. She lay there like heap of flesh but he was gone.' The old woman smiled a toothless smile of satisfaction. 'The devil was gone.'

'Then what happened?' Una was trembling, she daren't even look at Joan.

'I told Frankie what I'd done. I told him I'd killed the devil.'

'What did he do?'

'He cried. He said we had to keep it a secret or I'd be in trouble. He took her away. He was still crying when he came back but he said he'd hidden her where nobody would ever find her.' The faraway look came back into the old woman's pale eyes. 'His tears were for me. He did it for me.'

'Have you confessed this, my dear?' asked Joan.

'Confess? Why would I confess? It's not a sin to kill something evil, it's our duty!'

'What about her suitcase?' asked Una. 'What happened to that?'

'He burned it in the back garden.' She looked from Una to Joan and back. 'Can I go home now?'

'I think it's safe to say you'll be leaving here tomorrow,' Una told her. She took Joan's elbow and led her friend out onto the landing, closing the door behind them. Once outside, Joan switched off the voice recorder and the two friends slowly made their way down the long staircase. When they got to the reception desk, Marie was on the phone so she waved them off. Outside, the rain had let up. They got into Joan's car and sat quietly for a moment. Both were exhausted. It was Joan who spoke first.

'She couldn't have him,' she said, 'so she wasn't going to let someone else have him. It's a motive as old as man himself, unrequited love and jealousy.'

Una nodded. 'Compounded by an unstable mind,' she said, 'it was always going to be a recipe for disaster.'

The two friends travelled home in silence.

CHAPTER 19

The two women sat drinking a well-earned cup of tea in Una's kitchen. 'I'd bet my last custard cream the priest was behind it,' said Una, blowing on her tea to cool it.

'Do you think he really intended to run away with Kitty?' asked Joan.

'We'll never know for certain, but I'd say it was wishful thinking on the girl's part.'

'What makes you think that?'

Una smiled affectionately at her friend. 'You're a romantic Joan. In your mind, they were a pair of star-crossed lovers caught in a tragedy beyond their control, a Romeo and Juliet scenario. I'm a realist. I see a young man with power and influence who took advantage of an innocent country girl. When he found out she was pregnant, it presented him with a dilemma.'

'But Concepta confessed....'

'Tell me this, Joan. If someone is stabbed, do you blame the knife or the person who wields it?'

'I'm not with you, Una.'

'Look, Father Delaney knew perfectly well how Concepta felt about him. Those sort of men are always aware of the effect they have on women and they use it to their advantage. He also knew the poor woman was mentally unstable. He realised that if she thought he was giving up the priesthood and leaving her, it would tip her over the edge. I think he told her he was going away forever with Kitty, then left her to do her worst. Like lighting the touch paper on a firework then standing back to watch it explode.'

'Well I think that's a bit of a reach on your part.'

'He was very quick to dispose of the body. He could have easily said it was a tragic accident, that she'd tripped and fallen down the stairs.'

'Perhaps he panicked.'

'Perhaps he did, but he made sure he burned her suitcase the next day, didn't he?'

'I still think your theory is a little far-fetched.'

'Well, I doubt we'll ever find out the truth now,' sighed Una 'Loose ends, Joan, I don't like them.'

'I know, dear. Listen, I have to dash. A man's coming to take my rugs away for cleaning and he'll be here any minute.'

'Alright. Leave the voice recorder with me, will you? I want to listen to it a few more times, try and read between the lines.'

Una stood alone in the kitchen and looked at the recording device in her hand. It was six days since Kitty's body had been found in the bog. Joan had been convinced that the mystery was solved but she wasn't so sure. She opened the door of a press and put the device on a shelf. She would listen to Concepta's testimony tomorrow when her mind was clearer. Right now she needed something familiar, something routine to take her mind off the extraordinary events of the day. She went through to the parlour and switched on the TV, just as the theme music to Emmerdale began.

*

The next day was uneventful. Joan came for tea mid-morning, as usual, but the subject of the bog body was barely mentioned. Each had her own belief and they were never likely to know the full facts so what was the point of debating it? When Joan left, Una set up the laptop at the kitchen table and began to record the events of the previous day. It was late afternoon by the time she had finished and she read back through what she'd written. She was pleased with it.

'Move over Miss Marple,' she said out loud, 'Mrs. Murphy's in town.'

She printed off three copies on an old machine that Aine had brought from work. She rolled up one copy and shoved it inside a hollow Child of Prague statue that stood on the window sill in the parlour. She took down the Sacred Heart picture from the kitchen wall and taped a second copy to the back, before repositioning the picture over its flickering red lamp. The third copy she placed on top of the voice recorder that she'd left on the mantle over the fire.

*

It was a week now since Kitty's body had been discovered. The weather was typical of early Autumn in Ireland. Lashing rain followed bright sunshine which gave way to more rain, interspersed with a rainbow here and there. Una sat at the kitchen table thinking about Aine. Her week was up and she would have to tell her granddaughter everything today, but she still couldn't shake those loose ends out of her head. She hadn't seen the Mercedes since she'd blocked it in. She hadn't seen her own car since then either come to that, but she'd had a call from the car pound to say they had it there.

A loud rap on the front door made her jump. It couldn't be Joan, she always came in by the kitchen door and she never knocked.

The damp weather was affecting Una's joints and she had to haul herself up from the chair. She walked stiffly through to the hallway. *Growing old's not for the faint-hearted*, she thought to herself as she opened the door. A tall young man stood outside in the rain. He was wearing an unfashionable black fedora hat and a long black overcoat. Una looked past him and saw the Mercedes parked outside. She smiled.

'Come in,' she said, 'I've been expecting you.'

The young man returned Una's smile and stepped inside. He took off his hat and shook it, then unbuttoned his coat to reveal a priest's collar. 'So you were expecting me?' His accent was well-bred Irish, not local.

'Yes. You owe me a hundred euro.'

'I do?'

'Yes, Father. That's what they're going to charge me to get my car out of the pound.'

He was still smiling. 'It's Monsignor,' he said. 'Monsignor McCarthy and I'll have your car returned to you tomorrow. I've got to give it to you, Mrs. Murphy, that was a very clever ploy, blocking my car in so I couldn't follow you. And disguising yourselves as sisters so that Concepta would confide in you, well.... that was a stroke of genius.' Una wasn't a bit surprised that he knew her name.

'Cup of tea, your Grace?'

'Yes please, Una. May I call you Una?' His perpetual disingenuous smile was starting to annoy her.

'Do you have a first name?' she asked him.

'It's Terrence.'

'Very well. Since we'll be negotiating as equals, you can call me Una and I will call you Terrence.'

The smile slid from his face. 'What makes you think I'm here to negotiate?'

Una laughed. 'I doubt very much that you're here for my wit and repartee.' She switched on the kettle and motioned towards the parlour. 'Go through,' she said. 'I'll bring in the tea when it's ready.'

A few minutes later, she carried a tray into the parlour to find the priest standing in front of the fire with her typed notes in his hand.

'You do realise that none of this would hold up in court, Una,' he said. She glanced over at the Infant of Prague to see the statue lying on its side. 'Yes, I have that copy too,' he said, waving the second set of notes. 'I thought you'd be more creative in choosing your hiding places. We all know the Infant is every Irish woman's safe deposit box.' Una set down her tray on the coffee table and joined him in front of the fire.

'And how would you know what would or wouldn't hold up in court? Are you an expert in legal matters?'

'As a matter of fact, I am. I studied law at Oxford.'

'Really? I'm impressed.'

She took the notes from him, then folded them and placed them over the voice recorder, surreptitiously switching on the device. 'It's not the law courts that concern the Church in this matter though is it, Terrence? This has all the ingredients of a public relations nightmare and what I have could be very damaging.'

'In the current climate, it could be explosive. What is it you want, Una? Money?'

'I don't want anything for myself, I'm happy the way I am. But my granddaughter wants to study law. I want a place secured for her at law school and I want her fees paid.'

'Aine, isn't it?' Una nodded. 'Very well, consider it done.'

'I don't want Detective Inspector Quinn's career to suffer over this case. I don't want him to be made a scapegoat.'

'I'll take care of it.'

'I want Kitty's body returned to her nephew and I want her buried on sacred ground at the Church's expense, headstone included.'

'Ah now that could present a problem. She's scheduled to be cremated on Friday.'

'You'd better get on the phone so, Terrence.'

'Very well. Anything else?'

'Yes. I want the truth.' The clergyman's expression became sombre.

'Bishop Delaney made a statement on his deathbed, ' he said. 'It wasn't told in the manner of a confessional so it would be admissible in a law court. You weren't far off in your conclusion, Una. He was there the night Miss Egan knocked on the door of the parochial house, and he did push her down the steps in a fit of rage. But then he put Concepta's stocking around the girl's neck and managed to convince the poor addled woman that she'd caused the fall.'

They stood in silence for a moment. 'So you see,' he continued, 'those are the facts, but there's absolutely nothing you can do with them. It's your word against mine, what I believe the Americans call a Mexican standoff.'

'You're wrong,' said Una. 'In a Mexican standoff we'd have a gun to each other's head.' She lifted the papers off the recorder. 'And I seem to be the only one with a gun.' She brandished the device like a sword. 'When you have fulfilled all your promises, I'll destroy my paper notes and send you the hard drive on my computer. I'll send you this too, but you'll have to replace it because it's not mine.'

He held out his hand. 'You are as shrewd a negotiator as you are a detective, Una,' he said. The handsome young man shook hands with the portly old woman, then he left.

*

The Bog Body

It was the first Saturday in November that Una sat at her kitchen table drinking tea and pondering over the changes that had happened over the last month.   Her best friend now compiled her shopping lists with a state-of-the-art recording device, complete with voice recognition. Kitty was buried in the village cemetery under a beautiful marble headstone, and Concepta was getting the help she so badly needed at Dublin's top psychiatric hospital. Aine had been surprised and delighted to be accepted into Trinity College's School of Law and her grandmother..... well, Una had the truth and that's all she'd ever wanted.

'Nan.'

'Yes, pet?'

'The florist just delivered a dozen roses for you. Who's Terrence?'

W.A. Patterson

The Bog Body

Made in the USA
Columbia, SC
25 November 2020